Library
Brevard Junior College
Cocoa, Florida

Nothing Matters

Nothing Matters
and other Stories
By Herbert Beerbohm Tree (1853–

Short Story Index Reprint Series

BOOKS FOR LIBRARIES PRESS
FREEPORT, NEW YORK

First Published 1917
Reprinted 1970

INTERNATIONAL STANDARD BOOK NUMBER:
0-8369-3687-6

LIBRARY OF CONGRESS CATALOG CARD NUMBER:
70-132130

PRINTED IN THE UNITED STATES OF AMERICA

FOREWORD

The welcome accorded to a book of essays entitled "Thoughts and After-Thoughts," emboldens me to bind together these stories, written in holiday hours.

As epilogue to this Variety Show of Life, I have included "The Importance of Humour in Tragedy," a presidential address delivered at the Birmingham Midland Institute in 1915.

While I am conscious that this book may not add to the reputation of its author (man cannot add to that which he hath not) I cherish the hope that it may be acceptable as a tribute to the fund for actors disabled in the war. To these comrades it is hereby dedicated as a labour of love from afar.

H. B. T.

California, 1916.

CONTENTS

I. Nothing Matters
    PAGE
1. The Best Man 1
2. The Madonna of the Yellow Rose 10
3. "And He did Eat of It" . . 26
4. The Shadow of Joy . . . 32
5. "Let Him now Speak—or for ever Hold his Peace" . . . 46
6. "The Evil that Men do" . . 58
7. The Pity of it 65

II. The Mystery of Howard Romaine
1. Strange Disappearance of a Suicide 75
2. The Mystery Deepens . . 78
3. His Own Obituary . . . 83
4. What is Fame? 85
5. His Own Body-Snatcher . . 94
6. Hush! 98

III. The Stuffed Mouse . . . 103

IV. The Stout Gentleman . . . 111

V. The Lament of a Lilliputian Twin 125

VI. The Ultimatum, or Every Man has his Price 137

Contents

		PAGE
VII.	THE FATAL FAIRY	149
VIII.	CHAPTER ONE—A FRAGMENT . .	163
IX.	THE CUCKOO CLOCK . . .	177
X.	GOD IS GOOD	197
XI.	THE IMPORTANCE OF HUMOUR IN TRAGEDY	205

Nothing Matters

CHAPTER I

THE BEST MAN

HE was the last of his race; at the age of twenty-one he had inherited a baronetcy and the family estates; he had been sent to Eton; he had duly graduated at Oxford; he had diligently gone through a London season; his name was on the list of the most orthodox clubs. His education as a man of the world was in fact complete; yet he had emerged from the social machine a child of Nature. From an early age he had been somewhat reserved. Owing partly to a constitutional shyness and partly to an acquired habit of self-absorption, he shrank from contact with the great world. A long, shambling man with straight hair, a man whose eye seemed to be looking through the town to some distant meadow beyond; homespun, unobservant, he was one of those self-conscious beings who always say less than they think, for fear of saying more than they feel. At the age of thirty-five he had developed into a country

Nothing Matters

gentleman with a taste for practical engineering, and was supposed by all his acquaintance to be a convinced bachelor. There was, indeed, a self-imposed reason for the celibacy of this man in whose ancestry there was a taint of madness—many an Inglefield had been stricken with melancholia; and the last of his race had always had a misgiving lest the tragic fate which had afflicted his forbears should cast its shadow on his own life and on the lives of his progeny. At an early age he had consulted a celebrated specialist, who had assured him that if no suspicious symptom asserted itself before he had approached middle age, he might with safety marry. To perpetuate his race is the natural instinct of man, and the hope that his name and fortune should pass to a child of his own had often possessed Inglefield's mind.

He had little personal ambition. With every inducement to throw himself into the stream of public life, he had declined to prostitute his ideals to political expediency; he had not sufficient pliability of character to sacrifice his convictions in response to the mighty throbs of the great heart of the nation.

He had not the worldliness to recognise that for all practical purposes a man is not what he is, but what he appears to be; nor had he the genius of the courtier—an infinite faculty of not being bored.

The Best Man

This contempt of the world, which many attributed to indifference, sprang in reality from the depths of an outwardly calm but inwardly volcanic nature, and showed itself even in the cut of his clothes, which looked as if they had been made for some knight of the Middle Ages who had been pressed into the custom of a fashionable West End tailor.

Such a man was George Inglefield.

Not so his friend Guy Barrimore, who united in himself the qualities in which the elder man was deficient, and in whom were strongly developed those graces of the mind which are denied to the tougher fibre of the well regulated. To Guy the power of self-denial was practically an unknown quantity. He was a slave to his sense of beauty; to him luxury was a necessity. He had been George's fag at school, but such was the power of the younger man that he governed the elder by sheer amiability of temper, and punctually consumed the good things which were regularly consigned to his chum. This friendship, which was based by the one on reverence and by the other on affection, continued unabated during the manhood of these two. Such friendship is known to few dwellers in great cities. In a jostling capital where each gap is readily filled up friendship has an insecure foothold. Men become intimate in a day; club friendships are struck up

Nothing Matters

in an hour. In the strife of London life we lose a friend, say " Poor fellow ! " and call for the waiter to complain that our chop is underdone. The life of a great metropolis has all the heartlessness of a battlefield. Friendship requires for its growth the solitude of the wilderness. Freemasonry, no doubt, had its origin in the desert.

The sympathy between these two men was probably due to the aloofness which characterised their widely different natures. Each in his way was lonely. Happy is the man who has one friend.

George Inglefield was never tired of admiring the brilliant qualities of his vivacious companion, and lost no opportunity of urging him to turn his many-sided talents to practical account. Guy in his light-hearted way deprecated what seemed to him the exaggerated praise of his less imaginative comrade, and regarded himself and his literary work with a modesty which was one of the charms of his versatile nature. He asked of life nothing but to be allowed to enjoy it. " Ravish the moment lest you perish in the hour," he would say. He had made an early marriage which turned out unfortunately for his wife and for himself. It was said that there were faults on both sides ; be that as it may, Guy took the burden of blame on himself. In his own queer way he excused his flitting temperament to a friend by lamenting that he resembled the cherubim which

The Best Man

have only wings—they lack the wherewithal to repose !

To a quick and sympathetic disposition Guy added a wit which never wounded, for he shrank constitutionally from hurting, less perhaps from a deep consideration of others than from a sensitive organisation which made himself feel the pain he inflicted. He could not have hurt a woman's feelings any more than he could have crushed a blackbeetle—it was ugly. He was everything by turns, and everything sincerely; he had in him the potentialities of a saint and of a criminal —an æolian harp on which every passing wind of fancy, every gust of passion could play its own tune.

Such a man was Guy Barrimore.

His versatile nature enabled him to throw himself with ease into any mood. His quick sympathy for suffering had inspired in him views of life which would be called socialistic; while his innate love of refinement and repugnance to the outwardly ugly rendered him archæologically conservative. He had at one time lived the life of an ascetic, yielding himself up to the luxury of self-sacrifice. His soul had felt the throb of world-pity; his heart had revolted against the unrelenting, unfathomable logic which governs the world, and in his despair he had sobbed aloud, " There is no God."

Nothing Matters

One evening Guy entered George's chambers. His friend was in the act of sealing up a document.

"Hallo! what's the mystery?" cried Guy.

"I have been making a codicil to my will."

"What!" cried Guy. "Have you made up your mind to die?"

"No," said the other quietly; "I have made up my mind to marry."

"Good God, man! Whom?"

"Come in to dinner, Guy, and we'll talk things over."

The two friends sat down to table. George was an extremely reserved man, who only thawed under the influence of wine, and the dinner passed in a conspiracy of silence so far as the topic which engrossed them was concerned. Guy with his quick perception understood that the subject could only be broached under the mellowing influence of nicotine, and professed during the dinner to be entirely absorbed in a new incubator which had lately engaged his friend's energies.

Dinner over, the two men looked at one another.

"Well, and who is she?"

George blushed through a cloud of tobacco.

"She's a hospital nurse; we met in New York. She nursed me through my illness," he suddenly blurted out. A silence ensued during which both men puffed violently at their cigars.

The Best Man

" Is she English or American ? "

" Oh, English ! "

" Do you know her people ? " Guy asked.

" No ; I don't know her people."

Another and a longer pause.

" Do you know her antecedents ? "

" Antecedents ? How dare you ! " cried George.

Guy lapsed into a yet longer silence. It was time to light another cigar. He lit one.

" Capital cigar that, George."

" Yes," said the other.

" Do you know the brand ? "

" Exceptionales," George replied.

" Ah ! " rejoined his friend.

George coughed. A terrible sobriety fell upon both ; each felt the pulsation of the other's mind, and Guy diplomatically uncorked another bottle of wine. Suddenly George burst the bonds of self-consciousness, and pacing the room, poured out his heart to his friend.

" I know what you are thinking, but you don't know her ; when you do, you will see that I am right. You will be friends—I have told her all about you. You know I am not an impressionable man. To me this affair is not an episode ; it is my life—it is my past and my present and my future. Don't speak. Nothing you can say can change me ; she stands apart

Nothing Matters

from all other women I have known; I have not even questioned her about her past, and I would allow no one to question it."

Guy saw that to seek to stem the tide of George's passion would be to seek to dry up Niagara with blotting-paper. Such men cannot master their passions—they are engulfed by them. If they go " mucker " they rush headlong.

He who had run the gauntlet of the London marriage market, who had turned a deaf ear to the blandishments of designing dowagers, had fallen an instant victim at the feet of an unknown, friendless girl. What was it that had attracted this undemonstrative man in whose life the influence of women had been a strangely unimportant factor? Guy wondered, as he watched his friend, who had thrown up the window and stood with his broad back turned, gazing into the night. What was the subtle influence which had captured the heart and possessed the soul of this self-contained man? Was it the romance which work weaves round a woman? Was it rebellion against the thraldom of the social system? Was it that nameless perfume, that subtle atmosphere which surrounds some women, which intoxicates the senses and hypnotises the soul of man? Guy was too much of the world not to know that to tug at the strings of Love is only to tighten its bondage. He had

The Best Man

too great a reverence for his friend to wound his feelings by questioning the worthiness of the woman who had given a new beauty to his life. Rising from his chair, he went towards George, and putting his arm around his shoulder, said:

"Old man, forgive me! I wish you joy—Come and let us finish the bottle. Here's to the luckiest girl in England! I shall be at your wedding, George?"

"Yes, Guy; you shall be best man."

The two men took hands in a long grasp, and in the silent understanding of friendship they looked into each other's eyes.

"Now, Guy, you know why I neglected to have my hair cut," said George in his quiet manner.

Guy, laughing, threw back his head and passed his hand through his curls. It was a trick he had.

CHAPTER II

THE MADONNA OF THE YELLOW ROSE

BIG BEN was booming two as Guy issued from George's chambers in St. James's Square. In a meditative mood he sauntered towards his own rooms on the other side of St. James's Park. "Poor old George!" he kept on repeating to himself—why he hardly knew. They had talked much that night, and Guy could not repress a misgiving as to George's sudden and unaccountable resolve. He knew that with such men there is no going back; he knew that none are so liable to delusions as the hard-headed, the unimaginative. Most of the great mistakes of the world are made in the name of common sense. What sort of woman could this be who had changed the whole current of his life? George had reasons for keeping his engagement a secret; he had a hatred of the whole paraphernalia of marriage, and had already made up his mind that the wedding should take place in the little church attached to his property in Kent.

George Inglefield sailed for America the next morning, in order to dispose of his property in

The Madonna of the Yellow Rose

Virginia, where his mother resided, and whence he would return with her to make arrangements for his wedding. Guy started for the Continent, bound for the little town of Kreuzbrunn in the Bohemian Forest, whither he went to repair the ravages of a London season and to store up health for another campaign. His power of unswitching himself at will from any mode of life was one of the accomplishments of this many-sided man. To such men as Guy, men who live every moment of their lives, this power of unswitchment is the salvation of the nervous system, and Guy revelled in the luxury of laziness with the same energy which he threw into the active enjoyment of life. Thus he abandoned himself to the simple joys of this little sleepy town.

The society of his fellow-men always bored Guy, who, indeed, was never entirely at his ease with the male of his species. He could join in a club conversation, but the sporting shop tired him infinitely, and the average clubman's views on women irritated him. He found the society of the least attractive woman more engaging than that of the mess or club room. Here at Kreuzbrunn he gave himself up to a dreamy existence. Taking with him the Songs of Heine, he would pass whole afternoons in the woods. High up in one of the hills there was a little plot of ground which he had christened " No Man's Land."

Nothing Matters

Here by the side of a brook he would abandon himself to his thoughts ; here he would sit for hours, his senses lulled by the ripple of the water. The trunk of a tree had fallen across the brook ; there he would lie listening to the singing of the birds, watching the myriad tiny things in nature, allowing his favourite poems to glide through his mind. Detached from the world he would think out the great problems of life and death which force themselves upon us in solitude. In the solemnity of silence, beneath the stately pine-trees, he would look at the world with another mind, reviewing his past life, making new resolves, and swearing a truce to frivolity. This was his annual soul-cure. He had completed his three weeks, and was about to start the next day for Innsbruck in the Austrian Tyrol. To his club he telegraphed to have all letters and telegrams forwarded there.

Before leaving, he would pay a farewell visit to " No Man's Land."

It was a sunny forenoon, and Guy was at peace with all the world as he watched the sporting of the water-fly, the writhings of the tiny denizens of the brook. All nature seemed lapped in a happy calm. A gorgeous butterfly flapped lazily across the brook, and hovering above the stream stooped to kiss its own reflection, when, as a penalty of vanity, a sudden gurgle of water

The Madonna of the Yellow Rose

swept the dainty creature into its whirl. For a moment Guy watched the struggle of the frantic insect; and with a sudden impulse, regardless of his clothes, he went to its rescue. Gently he placed it on the palm of his hand; gradually he noticed signs of returning vitality; tenderly he gave it the warm sun rays; with his own breath he dried the draggled wings which at last, taking flight, carried their slender freight to the sky. His eyes followed its harmony of blue and silver swirling upwards. Suddenly it vanished through the leaves, when in its place, as if by magic, he beheld a rhapsody of red and gold—it was the face of a woman. For a moment he was uplifted into fairyland as by the wand of some magician; the butterfly seemed transformed into a goddess. Guy stared. No—it was a reality; there, peering through the leaves above the waterfall, was the face of a girl. She had evidently been a silent witness of his act. On her lips was a smile, half of thankfulness, half of amusement; in her eyes were tears of gratitude; on her cheeks was the blush of discovery. Two arrows darted from her eyes and flashed into his heart. He felt that a supreme moment of his life was striking—an impression which was destined never to fade. Both stood thus, gazing at each other. Then Guy, with shamefaced humour, lifted his hat and said:

Nothing Matters

"Gallant rescue of a butterfly!"

The face smiled a sympathetic understanding.

A yellow rose dropped in front of him, and the vision of the golden hair vanished. Was it a vision? Guy was standing in the water; the dream was complete—save for his wet boots. The man's first impulse was to make for the waterfall. Had not the vision thrown him a flower? Was it accident or design? He knew that the face was the face of an Englishwoman—its well-bred freedom told him that. After recovering his presence of mind, Guy ascended the little winding path leading up the rocks. Titania herself was not more invisible than the lady of the yellow rose. He wended his way home—his peace of mind was gone; his philosophy had been rudely disturbed; only one image filled his brain—the image of the face among the leaves.

"Who can she be?" he asked himself. "I can't rest till I know; the face was the face of an empress, or of a peasant woman, or of a madonna. I shall meet her—I know I shall meet her again."

The man began to run in sheer excitement, then stopped and laughed at himself, and ran again homewards through the sloping woods to Kreuzbrunn. Arrived at his hotel, he scanned the visiting-list without finding any clue. There were not many English or Americans at Kreuzbrunn, and most of these he knew. He caught

The Madonna of the Yellow Rose

the distant strain of the band playing; he hurried to the parade and walked quickly through the crowd of loungers, but he looked in vain for the face of the weeping madonna with the humorous mouth. He talked absently with his acquaintance. He remembered that a new play was to be given at the theatre that evening; he at once secured a seat—she might be there. He returned to his hotel to dinner, and absently helped himself to three portions of *truite au bleu*, and passed the cruet-stand with such persistency that a newly arrived American lady remarked to her taciturn husband that she thought the gentleman opposite must be travelling in mustard.

After dinner Guy made his way to the theatre; the impression was still vivid in his brain, and he asked himself whether he was not a little mad. He had often fallen in love, but there was something abnormal about his present state of mind. He went to the play—the curtain was up—he looked round the sea of faces, but the *one* face was not there. He regarded the stage with a vacant stare and left the theatre at the end of the first act.

He walked back to his hotel through the public gardens; he had given up the chase. As he passed the kursaal he paused for a moment to listen to the Hungarian band, whose wild strains were in accord with his own mood. Sitting down

Nothing Matters

on a garden seat, he lit a cigarette, and from that cool coign of vantage watched the gay scene within, where the many-coloured frocks of the women mingled with the uniforms of the soldiers. The Austrian officer waltzes as the nightingale sings, because he has nothing else to do.

Suddenly he sprang to his feet as there floated past the window a whirling vision of the face among the leaves. It was she—the same smile was playing on her lips—the same sadness was in her eyes. Guy stood transfixed. Again the vision passed the open window in languorous undulations, embraced by the usurping arm of Baron von Stumpel, a young Viennese officer. Guy at once entered the ball-room, paying his toll of half a florin at the doors. Evening dress is not *de rigueur* at these informal functions where the bourgeoisie of the town mingle with the visitors of all classes with an equality and a fraternity unknown to our more abrupt class distinctions. Guy saw from afar the now loathed form of Baron von Stumpel looming down, his spurs clanking aggressively in his triumphal approach.

"How dare he!" thought Guy, with the unreasoning scorn of a lover at a disadvantage.

At this moment the locked pair were passing. Suddenly the eyes of the madonna met his. There was the momentary widening of recognition; a flush told him that the unspoken

The Madonna of the Yellow Rose

flattery of the yellow rose in his coat had had its effect; its mate was gleaming in the breast of the woman who had unconsciously stopped on recognising the man of the woods.

The two stood opposite each other; some strange interchange of sentiment had passed between them—something subtler than the perfume of a yellow rose.

Baron von Stumpel looked round for the cause of this sudden halt. Guy bowed; the three stood for a moment perplexed.

"Do you know each other?" broke in the baron, thus rescuing the situation.

"No," said the lady quietly; "but if you wish it, you may introduce me to your friend."

"A countrywoman of yours, Miss——"

Guy did not catch the name—everything was a blur—things abstract and concrete seemed strangely merged. In such moments sight, sound, and thought are of one substance.

A curious etiquette obtains in this country—a code of honour at once freer and more precise, which is, in a sense, governed by a sword blade. Introductions are less formal, but it is said that if a lady refused to dance with an officer, the latter might consider this an insult to his uniform, and by way of vindicating his honour might challenge any male relative of the lady who happened to be within fighting distance. Guy

Nothing Matters

was not unacquainted with this greater freedom which is born of a severer code of honour, and at once took advantage of the situation by asking whether he might be permitted a dance, apologising for his unorthodox attire. Baron von Stumpel frowned as his companion's arm dropped lightly from his; but bringing his spurs together with a military click, he retired with as much grace as the situation permitted and left the Englishman the most perplexed, but the most happy man in Bohemia. A sudden shyness overcame Guy, who had the gift of blushing gracefully. Being struck dumb, he paid this silent tribute to the woman's beauty—it is the clumsy wooer who pays a direct compliment at first sight. To women there is something delicious in dazzling a man into bashfulness. Guy felt at a disadvantage when he remarked that it was a fine night. It is, as a rule, the woman who has the greater aplomb, being gifted with a larger subtlety in little things.

"I dropped a rose in the woods to-day. You must have found it."

Guy had recovered his self-possession.

"Then it was not a dream," he said quietly.

The band began to sob a slow mazurka.

"Were you alone to-day?" he asked.

"Alone? Oh, no."

The Madonna of the Yellow Rose

"Ah! of course not."

"Why of course not?" she asked.

Guy's self-consciousness had returned; he was vaguely hoping that Baron von Stumpel had not been an accessory to their improvised romance.

"Would you rather that I took you to your people?"

"I have no people," she said quietly.

"Oh! I beg your pardon. I thought you said you were not alone to-day."

The eyes of the madonna preserved their sadness; her mouth smiled.

"Shall we sit out this dance?" asked Guy.

"Yes, if you wish it."

"Pardon me, I did not quite catch your name—er—Mrs.——"

"Oh, no; I am sorry to say I am only 'Miss.' What made you think I was married?"

"How stupid of me! I suppose it was because—because you said your people were not here."

"It *was* rather daring of me to come here unchaperoned. But Baron von Stumpel promised to look after me. In America, you know, girls often go to dances with young men."

"Ah, indeed!" said Guy. "I should not have taken you for an American."

"Why?" asked the stranger.

"Oh, because you blushed."

Nothing Matters

"I suppose," said she, "blushing is an acquired habit, like most things," this with just a suspicion of an American accent, whether assumed or not Guy could not discover.

His cross-examination had not enlightened him as to the nationality of his enigmatic partner, who possessed the dignity and the good manners of perfect naturalness. Guy wondered whether she was a lady in the accepted sense, but then he reflected that this was almost an indignity—one might as well question whether the Venus of Milo was a lady.

Ten o'clock struck, and the madonna started to her feet.

"This is too bad. Baron von Stumpel promised that I should be home by ten," she said. "I must run across the gardens. I promised not to be later."

"But Baron von Stumpel is leading a cotillion ; it would be a crime against military etiquette to approach him at such a moment—a cotillion is not a thing to be trifled with."

The madonna looked distressed, bit her lip, and finally assented to being accompanied across the grounds by Guy, under a promise that he would explain her departure to the baron. Guy remarked that it might not look well for her to be escorted home by an officer in uniform.

The Madonna of the Yellow Rose

"I never thought of that," she replied.

"Will you think it a great liberty if I ask you a question. Was it Baron von Stumpel who was your companion of the woods?"

"Oh, no," the girl said frankly.

"Thank God!" muttered Guy to himself.

"It was one much dearer to me than Baron von Stumpel can ever be." The grey eyes glistened mischievously, the mouth curved humorously. "It was Siegfried."

"A hero, too, I take it," remarked Guy, with impertinent nonchalance.

"Yes; Siegfried is always by my side during my walks; you must make his acquaintance. He is a Dane. Here is my home, thank you; it was indeed kind of you to take care of me. Goodnight."

Guy did not move, but stood looking at the door through which the vision had vanished. It was a fine night; the moon was shining, and still he stood peering at the door for inspiration to clear up this mystery. He must have stood thus for ten minutes when he heard the opening of a lattice window above, and there appeared the head of a woman; the face was turned towards the sky—she did not see him; a liquid star started from its sphere and fell upon Guy's face. From that moment the man's soul was not his own.

Nothing Matters

"Who is Siegfried?" he asked himself as he threw open the shutters in the morning and allowed the sun to stream in. It was seven o'clock. His window commanded a view of the promenade where, their glasses in their hands, the pilgrims to the shrine of Kreuzbrunn were going through that species of faith-healing which is called "taking the waters." Guy watched the gay throng of dyspeptics as they wandered hither and thither to the tune of the band. Suddenly there flashed among the neutral-tinted crowd of heads a note of colour—it was the head of the madonna. Guy hastened into the fray; there like a pennant in a tournament he could distinguish the shining head of his lady-love. Soon he was by her side; she was alone, save for the presence of a huge Danish boarhound.

"Let me introduce you to Siegfried," she said gravely.

Guy felt relieved.

"I am surprised to find you among the valetudinarians — your cheeks belie you," he said.

"Oh, no," she replied. "I have been to buy my roses. I must have them every morning. I spend all my pocket-money in this way."

She was dressed in a simple fashion—there was not even an attempt at smartness, but her distinguished bearing and the curves of her figure

The Madonna of the Yellow Rose

made the woman in brown holland the most conspicuous form among the throng.

"Do you mind my walking by your side?" Guy asked.

"Oh, no; on the contrary, I felt rather awkward walking alone—these foreigners stare so," the girl replied ingenuously.

Two "smart" ladies of Guy's acquaintance passed at this moment. He noticed that they raised their eyebrows slightly, and he bowed in a half shamefaced manner.

"Who was that lady?" asked the girl.

"Oh, that was Lady Vulliamy."

"How beautifully she dresses! Is she very charming?"

"Yes; she is supposed to be very witty—she tells anecdotes with wonderful aplomb. She uses strong language with a better grace than any woman I know. She is most exclusive. She is here *en garçon*."

"I hate people of that sort, but I suppose she can afford to be vulgar."

Taking the girl's arm with the shamelessness of a boy, Guy led her to a seat under the trees. "Let us talk here," he said. Then he lighted a cigarette—she took his silver case in her hand. "May I hold this for you?" He knew that she loved him. He looked straight into her eyes—she looked straight into his; she seemed to read

Nothing Matters

his soul, and he hers; there was no secret between them—they understood; there was no need for words. He gave a little sigh; she dropped a yellow rose. "I shall call you Yellow Roses," he said, as he placed the trophy in his buttonhole.

How quick is the infection of the plague of love! Two human souls had met in space and clashing, became one. She was the elemental woman; he was just a man. The perfume of her body mingled with the scent of the roses; their incense intoxicated his being; he had conquered the world. Suddenly the young woman started up as the clock struck eight, and with military precision the band ceased to play.

"I am wanted," said the girl, as she made haste to go, looking anxiously towards the road.

He took her hand. "We meet to-night?" he asked.

"Yes."

"Dinner?"

"No; I am afraid I may not be in time for dinner. Do not wait for me; but I will come."

"Where?"

"At the Hohendorf on the hill; the Hungarian band plays there—we will listen to the music. Quick!" And she made her way towards an elderly lady in a bath chair.

The Madonna of the Yellow Rose

"Good-bye, Yellow Roses," said he.

"Good-bye, Butterfly," said she.

The cavalcade of the invalid in the bath chair, her companion of the yellow roses and the great Dane passed on. Guy stood rapt, expectant of the night.

CHAPTER III

"AND HE DID EAT OF IT"

THE night came.

The Hohendorf Restaurant is situated on a hill overlooking Kreuzbrunn. One of the delights of this peaceful Bohemian oasis, in which Guy spent many of the happiest hours of his life, was to breakfast, to lunch, and to dine under the trees of the little restaurants which dot the hills, where the food and the wine were always excellent, and where one could listen to good music at almost every hour. Guy repaired to the Hohendorf and ordered his dinner. One of his peculiarities was that he could not eat alone, and he refrained from partaking of his Vienna veal cutlet and compôte with an absent-mindedness which shocked the *maître d'hôtel* and caused the pretty waitress attired in the Bohemian national costume to make sympathetic inquiries " whether perhaps the waters did not agree with the gracious gentleman's stomach?" Guy's eyes were turned towards the pine trees through which Yellow Roses would pace forth to her tryst. " She will not come—she will not come," he repeated to

"And He Did Eat of It"

himself. At last—at last he caught sight of her lithe figure wending its willowy way swiftly through the forest trees—another minute, and she was by his side.

"Why so late? Have you changed towards me already? So soon?" he asked.

The girl looked at him with her sad eyes, more thoughtful, more wistful than before. The humorous curves of her mouth quivered.

"Changed? No; I do not think I could change, but——"

"But what, my rare one?"

"I have a telegram."

"From England?"

"No; from Rome. What shall I do—what shall I do?" she said, beating her knuckles together.

"Hush!" said Guy, as the serving-maid approached with a dish of river trout gaping to be eaten. The madonna consented to share the feast. The Hungarian band played a blasphemous little waltz. "Dear one," said he, "let's enjoy ourselves, and after we will mingle our remorse."

Yellow Roses laughed through her tears. "Yes," she said, "let's be happy to-night."

They ate and drank and were merry.

"Oh! by the way, who is the lady of the bath chair?" asked Guy.

Nothing Matters

"She is an English lady—a hypochondriac."

"And you?"

"Oh! I am the companion of the bath chair."

"I see," said Guy realisingly; "you earn your own living."

"Yes; I am the companion of the lady you saw—her name is the Honourable Miss Bittinger. I like to be independent, though to be sure I shall be rich some day."

"Soon?"

"Yes; perhaps very soon—that is what makes me unhappy."

Guy, who had known many loveless millionaires, reflected that women do not love men because they are rich—it is rather the other way; for a woman will mistrust herself lest she be giving herself to a man *because* he is rich, and love is so tender a plant that this very doubt will kill it.

The music had turned to a sad and wailing monotone.

"I may have to be leaving any day." She gave him her hand, and he kissed it. "I almost wish I had not met you," she added; "you make me too happy, you make me forget—this." The telegram was crushed in her hand.

"From someone who loves you?"

The girl nodded slowly.

"And He Did Eat of It"

"Someone you love?"

"I should," said Yellow Roses, "but you know—— Oh, let me go—let me go! I came to tell you, and I cannot tell you. I do not want to tell you. I do not want you to know."

"Tell me to-morrow," he said. "To-night, let us listen to what the music tells us."

They sat long with their hands clasped and listened to the palpitating syncopations of the gipsy band. They were transported on the vibrating wings of sound into a kingdom of their own —then there was a long silence. Suddenly they were awakened from their dream by the guttural voice of Baron von Stumpel. To their horror they realised that the baron was making his way towards their table, and he would inevitably join them.

"Quick!" cried Guy, and the girl stepped into the darkening forest.

Guy settled the bill and, raising his hat to the intruding officer, followed the figure of the girl. Hand in hand they walked down the sloping path toward Kreuzbrunn. The music spoke their thoughts. Each knew the other's secret, though no word of love had been spoken. The girl leant without shame on Guy's arm. He looked into her eyes—they were filled with tears; the mouth no longer curved humorously. Guy bent down and kissed her lips. All the world was changed;

Nothing Matters

she only sighed; love had come to her—such love as knows no pride, no shame, whose victory is surrender.

"It seems so long ago since yesterday," she said.

They found themselves on the margin of "No Man's Land"; they struck from the beaten path, and sat by the waterfall.

"What made you like me?" asked Guy.

"The butterfly," said the girl, as she pressed to her lips the bunch of yellow roses he had given her.

Her head dropped on his breast. They did not speak. The Hungarian music was throbbing and sobbing, and mocking and wailing, now cajoling, now melancholy, now hopeful, now despairing, now yearning, now passionate, now tragic; then suddenly breaking off to tell that life is a jest: "Nothing Matters!"

They listened, their hearts beating together. All the emotions that the gipsies felt were played on their heart-strings. The wild melodies told them of all the loves of all the Magyars, and of their remorse, and then again came the final theme, "Nothing Matters." They became one with the music. A solo stole out into the night. It began with a little plaint—like the wail of a new-born child—then it became gay and careless; quickly it passed into youth's yearnings, then burst into

"And He Did Eat of It"

full life, and always the refrain: "Nothing Matters." "I have lived, I have loved, I have lost, I have laughed—nothing matters! Life is tra-la-la-la! I gave her all my love—she laughed at me. She was my world; I cried my sorrows to the mountains; their echoes laughed, 'Nothing matters!' I wandered barefoot many miles; my feet bled—but for her. Out of my anguish I made songs for her—I sold them—for her; I wept and prayed night and day—for her; I gave her all I had—and she loved me. She spent my money and stole away to the town with another—I broke my violin over my heart. But the spring has come, and there is wine at the feast; and now I have stolen my enemy's fiddle—and there are many women. See—one is eyeing me now. Nothing matters!" And still the music seemed to say: "Let us be wise to-morrow—let us live to-night. It is madness—let us be mad. There is only one moment—that is the present; let us live for the present. What is eternity against this moment that is ours? There will be a time to repent—the moment is worth the pain of repentance. Nothing matters!"

The girl shivered in his arms.

The face of the moon was hidden by a cloud; the music was still; only a glow-worm lighted its tiny torch—only a nightingale trilled, and they were lovers as in Eden.

CHAPTER IV

THE SHADOW OF JOY

THE lights of Kreuzbrunn twinkled below, and towards them they wended their way through the night. There was a clearing in the woods, and here the two stood hand in hand, silent, looking at the stars, as millions of lovers had done before them, as millions of lovers will do after them. The vast firmament belonged to them; they were of it; they felt themselves above human laws. The woman's head drooped on Guy's shoulder and he kissed her hair, and the cool breeze fanned their faces. "Are you happy, dear one?" he asked.

"I was never so happy in my life—I shall never be so happy again," she answered.

They sat on a stone seat. On it was a carved inscription.

"What does that mean?" asked the girl.

"It was on this seat that the poet Goethe wrote his famous lines to Rest." Guy translated them for her: "They don't sound much in English, but they say something like this: 'The pine-tops are still, and the bird in its nest. Wait

The Shadow of Joy

but a little while; thou, too, shalt rest." And he hummed the music.

The church bell awakened them, eleven o'clock struck, and they made their way to the little house where Goethe once dwelt.

"I am home now—quick—speak low—to-morrow we meet?"

"In the afternoon at four—by the waterfall?"

"Yes." She took the bunch of flowers from his hand and pressed them to her bosom. They had reached her door.

"Now you have not told me all about yourself—to me you are only Yellow Roses."

"Perhaps better so, dear," she said; "but to-morrow I will tell you everything—all that was—all that is—all that will be. Meantime, my name is Mary—Mary Seton. And *your* earthly name, Butterfly?"

"My name is Guy."

"Guy—*what?*"

"Guy Barrimore."

The door was open; the girl stood there, looking at him and looking at him still; then without a word the door closed. Guy did not move. To him it seemed the eyes were still staring at him through the panel. After some minutes he turned homewards. "Mary Seton," he muttered. "Mary Seton—why did she look

Nothing Matters

like that? Women are curious." On that night of nights he lay down in his bed and slept the sleep of a child.

The next morning found Guy in high spirits, wondering how he should kill the hours that intervened between him and his tryst; but he outwore the hateful hours, and in lovers' time arrived at his destination before clock-strike. He forgot all about his visit to Innsbruck.

He made for the path above the waterfall, so that he might see her approach. There is no suspense so torturing as that which lovers feel. Guy stood and waited—and waited: the madonna made no sign. Then he sat down upon a mound and tried to possess his soul in patience by thinking of her wonder. He saw in every blade of grass some little emblem of her life; he heard in every stirring leaf some whisper of her soul. The minutes passed, with heavy steps; the shadows of the trees grew longer; a strange apprehension began to possess the man as he watched the minute hand race round its little dial. Moments became minutes, minutes became an hour—and still he waited. The lover's throat became dry with unrequited hope.

"Can she have lost her way?" he thought, and he called her name loudly. The silence mocked him. Darkness began to fall. Guy descended the little path leading to their trysting

The Shadow of Joy

place by the brook; there he found her message: the mossy slope was strewn with petals of yellow roses. His offering lay scattered at his feet. The man's heart stopped beating. What could it mean? He stood staring vacantly down. A premonition filled his mind. "What have I done? What has happened to her?"

The apprehension of ill is worse than the knowledge of ill. Tragedy is worse in imagination than its reality; it is the fear of death, not death itself, that appals us. The fear of fear is greater than fear itself. Then he recalled her manner when they parted; he wondered whether he had unconsciously hurt the woman who had given him her love. He remembered her staring, wordless farewell. A numb sense of guilt overcame him. "I must go to her—I must find her," he murmured to himself. He took one more look at the ravished flowers, and, stumbling through the woods, he made for home. He could not walk; he could only run, as fast as his feet would carry him, through the rain. In his self-absorption he had not noticed the thunderstorm which Nature, in a dramatic mood, had provided, as though to emphasise the storm within the man. On and on he ran through the woods. Suddenly there was a flash of lightning. He stopped instinctively. From the ground a black object rose with flapping wings—it was a

Nothing Matters

belated crow. " Mary, Mary," it seemed to caw as it disappeared into the darkness. " Mary, Mary," the omen resounded more faintly. " Mary, Mary," Guy echoed as, drenched to the skin, he resumed his way, groping through the dark woods. Behind him he seemed to hear footsteps tracking his own. He looked round. Fate hid behind a tree. He made straight for Mary's home. The concierge, smoking his evening pipe, was watching the storm. " Has Miss Seton come home ? " he asked.

" No ; Miss Seton is not at home."

Guy seemed to detect a note of armed neutrality in the man's tone, and thought it more diplomatic not to pursue the inquiry. Disconsolately he walked to his hotel. He asked if there were a letter—none. From his window he could see the house where Mary dwelt ; he would watch for her home-coming ; he waited till midnight— still no sign of her. That night he did not sleep. He invented a hundred plans in the waking hours that he might unravel the mystery. He evolved a hundred different theories that might give a clue to the riddle. These watches of the night are apt to appal even the free who suffer the remorse of uncommitted crimes. In this state men see as through a vista all the consequences of their acts—and Guy was not devoid of imagination ; he was not without conscience. For

The Shadow of Joy

every stolen joy such a man suffers a thousandfold. He could no longer bear the suspense; restless, he leapt from his bed and threw up the window. There he sat for hours gazing into the night, impatiently watching for the light that might chase the goblins of the dark. The reproachful dawn shimmered fitfully on the horizon. The sun rose with a bloodshot eye, bringing no comfort.

The thought suddenly came to Guy that the girl might have been desperate and taken her life. Once engendered, the suspicion grew till it became an obsession. He quickly dressed himself, determined that he would not rest until he had assured himself of the truth. The woman filled his whole being; the lover and the sportsman in him vied with each other, and passion intensified their enterprise. The man was on fire. Nothing else in life mattered: he would find her wherever she was. She had started out for the woods: he would search them first. Near No Man's Land was a sheer precipice along which a narrow path led to the waterfall. Might she have lost her footing and so have met her death? He went straight to the spot, arriving hot and out of breath, his tongue clinging to the roof of his mouth. If she were dead, if he found her, suspicion would inevitably fall upon him. The thought, a selfish one, only added to his anxiety.

Nothing Matters

No; she was not there. Again he visited the scene of their love, thinking that there he might find some written message which in his excitement he had overlooked. The withered rose leaves were the only evidence vouchsafed. For two hours, the perspiration pouring down his face, on a hot, steamy morning, he searched the woods in vain. Breakfastless, worn out in body, his brain aflame, Guy returned to his hotel. The reply he had received from the porter did not encourage him to question him further. To seek information of the lady whose companion she was might be to prejudice Mary Seton in her patroness's eyes—he could find no excuse for such inquiries from a stranger who could not justify them without compromising their object. Then it occurred to Guy that she might have left by train. He drove straight to the station and inquired whether a tall, striking, red-haired lady had been seen at the station on the previous night, either alone or with some companion. None of the station officials had noticed anyone answering to the description given. Suddenly the mysterious telegram from Rome flashed across Guy's mind. He went to the booking office. Had any ticket been sold for Rome on the previous evening? Yes, two first-class tickets for Rome had been sold to a young lady just before the train left. That was enough. Guy deter-

The Shadow of Joy

mined to take train for Rome that night. Before doing so, he called at Miss Seton's house to assure himself, and casually said to the porter:

"I understand the ladies started for Rome last night?"

"I do not know," replied the man; "they only said that if inquiries were made, no address need be given."

He went to his hotel, telegraphed to Innsbruck that all letters and telegrams should be forwarded to him to the Hôtel de l'Europe, Rome, and started on his journey to Italy.

In Rome he had little difficulty in finding the mortal abode of his quarry, for the first thing his eye lighted on in scanning the newspaper was the following fashionable intelligence: "The Hon. Miss Bittinger has arrived at the Royal Hotel, Rome." Without preparing his diplomatic errand, Guy impulsively called at the hotel. He waited in the hall, hoping that accident might favour him, giving himself the air of a dawdler passing the time over a cigar and lemon squash.

He felt his mission was an awkward one. At last he summoned up courage to ask if Miss Mary Seton had gone out. The name was unknown to the hall-porter. Was the Hon. Miss Bittinger at home? The inquiry was made: the lady, who was an invalid, had left instructions not to be disturbed till after luncheon—the doctor was

Nothing Matters

with her now. Guy realised that his intrusion might not only be resented as unwarrantable by the lady, but also by the object of his devotion herself. Besides, a woman has a kind of royal prerogative in giving and taking away her favours. The lover's courage began to ebb. Uneventfulness in romance is more disconcerting than disaster. Guy passed the morning pacing up and down the hot pavement. He tried to interest himself in the sights of Rome; but all its ancient glories seemed as nothing. Julius Cæsar was no more to him than he to Julius Cæsar. It had always been his ambition to look upon the historic remains of ancient Rome and rehearse in their contemplation the great deeds of the mighty tyrants who swayed its destinies and made and unmade empires. Only one picture occupied his mind. Thus will a little woman fill the world, unpeopling it. Was not Cleopatra thus? All the great lovers from Marc Antony down to Milton Perkins were so undone: " 'Twas the female of his species laid Milton Perkins low." Love's restlessness was upon him. Things towards which one has a tendency come to one. To the humorous, life will become humorous. To him who seeks money—money comes. The botanist goes forth and finds his destiny among herbs. So to the lover comes love. Whatever we want in this world we get, whether it be title, wealth, or

The Shadow of Joy

quiet and content; but we have to sacrifice everything else for it. Given a fair intelligence and a strong will, every man reaches the goal of his ambition—if he does not die prematurely in the pursuit. Guy would compass his desire.

At last he determined upon a bold policy. He would write a letter to Mary Seton and leave it after luncheon with his own hands. A happy chance might even enable him to see the desired one herself. So he summoned up courage and wrote a little note, thus:

DEAR MISS SETON,—

I accidentally find myself in Rome. If I can render you any service, pray command me.

> Yours sincerely,
> GUY BARRIMORE.

My address is Hôtel de l'Europe. If I do not hear from you I shall understand that you do not recall a casual American acquaintance.

The note was sufficiently colourless, and the author prided himself on his tact in its composition.

At three o'clock Guy betook himself once more to the Royal Hotel, and nervously presented the letter addressed to Miss Mary Seton, c.o. the Hon. Miss Bittinger. As he entered the hotel the somewhat imposing presence of Miss Bittinger loomed into the hall—but the madonna

Nothing Matters

was not in attendance. The hall-porter at once took the letter to the elderly lady, saying :

"A gentleman gave me this letter, milady."

"Which gentleman ? " she asked, with arched eyebrows.

Guy bowed awkwardly, hat in hand.

"In Miss Seton's absence, may I open this ? "

Guy assented. The lady eyed him with that baffling self-possession which is the prerogative of the English aristocracy having passed the meridian of middle-age.

"Are you a friend of Miss Seton ? "

"An acquaintance."

"You met Miss Seton in America ? "

"Y-n-no," said Guy.

"Oh ! " said the lady.

"May I ask, are you American ? "

"Y-n-no. I had the pleasure of meeting Miss Seton at Kreuzbrunn."

"She did not tell me of her acquaintance—Mr. —Barrimore."

By this time Guy's aplomb had completely evaporated. The lady gave him a look such as one might cast on a private inquiry agent.

"I have a very high regard for that young lady ; indeed, I feel as a mother towards her."

"I am sorry if I have been indiscreet," faltered Guy.

The Shadow of Joy

" We are all liable to be indiscreet. Oh, by the by, if you are interested in Miss Seton, you may be glad to know that she left for London last night on a most important errand—in most excellent company. Good-bye."

The conversation was thus closed, and Guy withdrew with as much grace as the occasion allowed. Tripping over the door-mat as he left the hall, he noticed that it bore the word " Welcome " on it. Guy had never in his life felt such a sense of ignominy—never before had he tripped over a door-mat with " Welcome " on it. For the moment this feeling of outraged pride was stronger in him than was his chagrin at the news he had just heard. What could be the important errand ? Who was the " excellent company " ? he wondered, not without a tinge of jealous apprehension.

He returned to his hotel, conscious that his dignity had undergone a certain shrinkage. But at the hands of a woman one does not feel the same degradation as one would feel a slight at the hands of a man. Humiliation is indeed at times something in the nature of a sacrificial homage we pay in worship, as the ancients lacerated their bodies to propitiate their gods. And after all, was not his error the error of chivalry ? In his dealings with men Guy was of a proud habit. He would feel a certain humility in the presence of even a flower-girl. But *she* was gone—gone, perhaps for ever, out of his life!

On entering his hotel a telegram was put into his hand. It read thus:

Forgive, and when we meet forget.—MARY.

The message had been sent from Frankfurt railway station, and was addressed to the hotel at Kreuzbrunn, thence to Innsbruck, whence it was redirected to Rome. Guy kept on repeating the words, " And when we meet forget." She who had fled from him could speak of their meeting again! Could it be that she was playfully, wilfully torturing him? No, he thought, women torture when they love: love by torture is with women almost a sensual indulgence. Men hurt—but with a difference; they torture unconsciously through selfishness; while with many women—even virtuous women—torture is a definite expression of love. It is a kind of *auto-da-fé* through whose ordeal they will demand a man shall pass with love unscathed. This Guy knew from an expert observation of womankind.

The message from Mary Seton seemed to him the mere mockery of a flirt. A new mood came upon him. He laughed at himself. That he, who knew the whole gamut of the art of love—that he, who had gone through every phase of this affliction of adolescence, should now be subject

The Shadow of Joy

to its onslaughts in so virulent a form seemed to him almost ridiculous. So he betook him to a Bohemian restaurant, joined a group of merry journalists, insisted on being their host, and ordered an excellently selected feast, whose *pièce de résistance* was *bouillabaisse*. He was the soul of the party, recited Verlaine to his guests, and drank late into the night, listening to the band playing Offenbach's operettas, and laughing at the gods made fools by love. At dawn he rang the hotel bell, gaily humming a tune from " Belle Hélène." Nothing matters! The cessation of suffering is itself a joy—wine is the bath of sorrow, and laughter the vanishing point of despair. Turning his sorrows into copy he dashed off a sonnet to " The Madonna of the Yellow Rose," and went to bed. Never Bacchus slept more soundly.

CHAPTER V

"LET HIM NOW SPEAK—OR FOR EVER HOLD HIS PEACE"

GUY was awakened in the morning by the arrival of a bundle of belated letters which had been sent on from Innsbruck. With them was a telegram from George. It was dated from London, and readdressed from Innsbruck:

Just heard at club you are at Innsbruck. Did you not get my letters? Wedding Wednesday next, St. Margaret's, Westminster, at half-past twelve. All sorry if best man had no wedding garment, but fear too late. Telegraph immediately.

Guy leapt from his bed and rang for the Continental Bradshaw, from whose almost Athanasian incomprehensibilities he managed to decipher that a train would leave Rome in three-quarters of an hour and enable him to reach London at half-past eleven on the very day of the wedding. To bathe and dress himself, and to pay his bill, was the work of half an hour. He arrived at the station just in time to catch the train, but too late to send a telegram to George. Soon Guy was hurtling towards home with an

"Let Him Now Speak—"

eager expectancy of seeing his friend, and of being by his side in one of the great moments of his life. "What," he thought, "is the passing love of a woman compared with the friendship of a lifetime?" He cursed the fate which had not only given him many torturing hours, but which might be the cause of his defaulting from his friend. "How many friendships have been sacrificed to a woman!"

In the train Guy read a mass of correspondence, among which were two letters from George, telling him of his plans: that his mother had fixed the day of the wedding as being that on which her own marriage had taken place, and that he wished to indulge her in this maternal whim. George Inglefield had wished that the wedding should be quietly performed at the little church at Arlington; but women love spectacular weddings, and George's mother was no exception. Guy banished his own self-preoccupations in thinking of his friend; by sympathy with others do we effectually counter-weight the burden of self-pity. He wondered what kind of woman would she prove to be who was the chosen of this chosen among men. He passed in review their two lives whose meshes had been so uninterruptedly interwoven, and pictured to himself the happiness of the woman who was privileged to be loved by this rare man. He re-

Nothing Matters

flected that George was the only wholly good man he had ever met in life. In books one meets many such, but one somehow feels that they are only a concession to the unintelligence of the reader. He had never known George Inglefield do any act that was selfish or mean or greedy or self-righteous. How wonderful must be this woman who had influenced this man's life inevitably, unalterably, unreasoningly, insanely perhaps. It is useless to argue, to logicise with such passions; you might as well seek to put out the flame which leaps from such natures as seek to put a stop to an earthquake by writing to *The Times*. Men's lives are governed by their character—and character is destiny.

Such thoughts filled Guy's mind until his arrival in Paris. There he dispatched a telegram to George telling him he was on his way home to attend the wedding. On reaching Calais he found, to his dismay, that a fog was overhanging the sea and might cause the boat to be delayed in crossing. Ill-luck seemed to be dogging his footsteps, and he began to feel a vague foreboding that unsettled his mind. On arriving at Dover the boat was an hour behind its time, and he at once dispatched a telegram telling George of the mishap, but that he still hoped to reach the church in time to perform his duties. The remainder of the journey passed uneventfully

"Let Him Now Speak—"

enough, and at a quarter past twelve the train steamed into Victoria Station. Guy at once made for his chambers, arrayed himself in a frock-coat, and with the aid of a pair of white gloves and a gardenia was an immaculate best man; he hailed a hansom cab, and arrived at the church door a quarter of an hour after the appointed time. The ceremony had already begun, and he felt a lump in his throat as on entering he heard the hymn sung by the choir of St. Margaret's. A solemnity seemed to grip his mind and body in its grasp; it was one of those moments which we experience all too rarely as life advances into drabness and we have discarded the many-coloured garment of our youth.

Guy slowly, nervously, and reverently made his way through the middle aisle and approached the altar. Though he could not see the faces of the bride and bridegroom, their backs being turned, he gently laid his hand on George's shoulder, and the friend knew the touch of the friend. Guy looked through brimming eyes into George's, where reigned a great solemnity. Then he turned towards the bride; her face was veiled, but he at once realised the beauty of her outline. A strange sensation as of the scent of flowers of long ago overcame him.

The woman lifted her bowed head. Guy

was struck as if by lightning. For the moment Mary stood before him. Then the veiled head was turned away. No; it could not be she—it was a mere hallucination—a vision of the woman who had filled his whole being. And yet——

As he was wondering, the perfume of yellow roses stole upon his senses, and he seemed to swoon. He neither saw nor heard; sight and sound were blended as in a mist of silence, through which the drone of the clergyman's voice was as a tolling bell sounding from afar. "If any man—can show just cause—why they may not —be joined together—let him now speak—or else hereafter—for ever hold his peace."

These words emerged from the dimness with an unnatural clangour, beating like a brazen hammer on Guy's brain. He was awakened from his delirium by a woman's clear voice, saying these words: "I, Mary, take thee, George, to my wedded husband, to have and to hold from this day forward, for better, for worse, for richer, for poorer, in sickness and in health, to love, cherish, and to obey, till death us do part——"

It was the voice of Mary Seton!

Guy was restored to the reality of things around him; he visualised with an almost exaggerated clearness that he was officiating as "best man" at the wedding of George Inglefield, Baronet,

"Let Him Now Speak—"

and of Mary Seton, spinster. He saw George put a ring upon the fourth finger of the woman's left hand. Then the Lord's Prayer was spoken, and they were made man and wife in the name of the Father, and of the Son, and of the Holy Ghost.

Guy clearly heard the words, "Those whom God hath joined together let no man put asunder." Then the bride lifted her veil and she and Guy were face to face. The man did not move; he stood as a thing of stone; and the face was the face that he saw on the night of their parting; at her breast was a bunch of yellow roses; her eyes were still astare, her nostrils taut, the curves of her mouth were quivering. Then came into her face the look of the message: "Forgive, and when we meet forget." The colour had gone from her eyes, the lithe figure swayed, but George gently supported her. The quivering form regained its poise; and the look on Guy's face was that of a soul in anguish. And soon the music burst forth afresh as of the opening of a great wound, as George Inglefield, with his lady leaning on his arm, walked towards the vestry; and Guy followed like a man staggering in unholy wine. In the vestry they signed their names in the register; friends and acquaintances offered their felicitations to the bridegroom; women clustered round the bride demanding the

Nothing Matters

name of her dressmaker. And Guy was for ever another man.

Great as was his agony, a greater was in store. His impulse was to rush from the room—into the open air, and to be lost in the great forest of the city; but George took his arm and said: "You and Mary must be friends—I forgot you had never met." Guy took Mary's hand mechanically as strangers do. His face twitched nervously.

"Old man," said George, "you look ill! What is the matter?"

Guy at once caught at the trapeze of a desperate lie.

"Yes," he said; "I am ill—I am ordered abroad at once. I am sorry—I must go."

"You are going away?"

"I will write to you, George. Don't worry about me—they say I shall be all right in a few months."

"But," urged George, "you must promise to pay us a visit at Arlington. I have fitted up a suite that is to be yours; it is to be known as 'the Guy wing.' There will be nobody but ourselves; we shall pass our honeymoon there. You must not refuse."

Guy hesitated, seeking wildly but vainly for an excuse. As George turned to talk to the clergyman the woman seized Guy's hand, and said, quickly:

"Let Him Now Speak—"

"You must come. I will never ask you again—I understand, but you must come—just this once. For God's sake, promise!"

Guy, in dissenting, half consented, and with staring eyes found his way into the streets, wandering he knew not where. It must have been St. James's Park, for he was vaguely conscious that the surrounding colour was green. He wandered thus for hours, and at length found himself on the Embankment, the home of lost souls; he dimly realised that it had been raining, for his clothes were wet; he stumbled against a lump of human flesh, a poor, degraded specimen of London's "submerged tenth." He looked at the form with an awakening consciousness; the man was casting his head from side to side, looking for cigar-ends or other scraps discarded of men. And Guy envied this careless derelict of fortune. "Lucky devil," he murmured with a laughing sigh, as he stared at the passing river, lashed with rain. Dusk had fallen—but not oblivion.

There set in upon Guy a kind of moral neuralgia which he sought to benumb by drink and by drugs, waiting for the day of his visit to Arlington to come. No other thought than that of George and his wife occupied his brain; he tried to gamble at his club, but he revoked with such frequency that he had not the hardi-

Nothing Matters

hood to pursue the game at the expense of his partners. He went to the play; he saw the actors without regarding them—he heard them without listening.

At night he would wake at the ghostly flapping of a blind; he would wait for the recurrent torture of a rattling window. He would listen for hours to the tick-tack of the clock, till he seemed to hear the rhythmic shuttle of Fate weaving its relentless web.

The day came of his visit to Arlington; there he arrived without luggage in time for dinner, explaining that on the following morning he had to leave for Spain, where his presence was necessary to grapple with certain financial difficulties that had arisen in connection with his property. He ate and drank with forced gaiety; never tasted ashes and gall more bitter-dry. In the course of the dinner George rallied Guy as to the vagueness of his Continental whereabouts. He had only contrived to ascertain his Innsbruck address at the club. He himself had been to Rome with his mother, and had telegraphed to Mary to join them there; it was in Rome that his mother and Mary first met, and they all journeyed to London together. His mother's old friend, Miss Bittinger, had very kindly insisted on chaperoning Mary on her journey. Guy refrained from telling George of his own expe-

"Let Him Now Speak—"

dition thither. Despair, wine, the fierce inward conflict of clashing emotions, now opened the floodgates of his speech. He talked brilliantly to stifle his own tragic thoughts and compelled himself to an exaggerated flippancy; laughter long and loud filled the dining-hall. George observed the change in Guy, and when the two friends were alone with their cigars he kindly but gravely upbraided him for the first time for the tendency he had often noticed before of Guy's too free indulgence in wine. The younger man promised to "pull up" and to devote himself to his literary work which he had sadly neglected of late. Alas! he had no healthy outdoor hobby—he could never bring himself to kick a football when it was down.

George could not help feeling that there was a certain estrangement in Guy's manner which he could not account for, except on the score of his friend's health or his financial anxieties. He put his arm round Guy's shoulder, saying:

"Old man, remember that if you need any sort of help in your Spanish enterprise you must make me your banker: you never had a head for business affairs. Why not abandon this wild-goose chase—leave your 'castles in Spain,' and settle down for good as a respectable poet with a stake in the country?"

Guy laughed, threw back his head, and

Nothing Matters

passed his hand through his hair, as was his trick of custom. Then he thanked his friend gravely, and, looking at his watch, said he had only just time to catch the last train to London. Then Mary said:

"You must let me see you to the gate, Mr. Barrimore. We have hardly had a word."

They walked down the sloping ground through the trees as they had walked once before in the seeming long ago. For a brief while neither spoke; presently he said:

"Good God, what is to become of us? We must never meet."

Mary spoke. "I didn't know—how could I know? I had to marry—I knew that night that you were not free. I know he is the best man on earth. I will bear it all. Have I not that night to remember all my life? I know I am wicked—but I loved you—I love you now." And she threw her arms round his neck and kissed him on the mouth. The man thrust the woman from him.

"Listen! Mary, this must never be. He is my friend—our friendship is the only sacred thing in my life. That man is a thousand times more worthy than you or I can ever be. Try to be his comfort—and forget me. I swear I shall never give him cause to regret what he has done —I will never shame him or you or myself."

"Let Him Now Speak—"

They had reached the gate.

"Dear heart," said Mary, "you will be with me always."

Guy stared at her. Then she whispered in his ear words which the listening breeze did not overhear—and with a groan Guy stumbled into the darkness. They never met again.

CHAPTER VI

"THE EVIL THAT MEN DO"

ON the following day Guy took train "for Spain," sold his property for "a song," returned to London, and lived incognito at Hampstead, resolved to immerse himself in literary work. But the fever and the pain of his being would not be banished; he resorted to the habit of drugs as his only respite and nepenthe. He felt that his pen was losing its cunning, and he drifted into the backwater of self-indulgence and forgetfulness, rooting himself on the Lethe Wharf of Nirvana. So the months passed for Guy.

Happy in the new life which his marriage had brought him, George Inglefield was vouchsafed a supreme blessing to complete his joy—the hope of fatherhood. With his young wife he would pass the days in tender solicitude. Mary was grateful, and busied herself in the beautiful garden at Arlington tending the flowers, for George had taught her that to look on beautiful things would be to reflect an inward beauty in the mother and the life to be.

George Inglefield often speculated in his talks

"The Evil That Men Do"

with Mary as to Guy's whereabouts. His friend had not written, but he was led to suppose that Guy was still in Spain, and, as like many a literary man Guy was a notoriously bad correspondent, his silence did not cause surprise.

We who inhabit London are always being reminded that the metropolis is a poor hiding-place. One day George, having come up from the country to attend a directors' meeting, saw what seemed to him a familiar yet unfamiliar figure—that of a man leaning on a stick and walking somewhat unsteadily. George remarked a curious contraction at the back of the man's neck. The ears were of an anæmic transparency—signs which George had often noticed in those on whom death had laid his hand. He touched the shoulder of the man, who gave a shuddering cry as one whose nerves are shattered. It was Guy! What a change the months had wrought. The face was haggard, and the mouth twitched. George looked into the pallid face from whose eyes the light had gone and took Guy's hand. It was hot and dry, and the lips writhed the old smile.

"Why, Guy, you truant, how long have you been back? Why haven't you been to see us?"

Guy rambled that he had only been back a day or two, and wanted to get fit before he looked

Nothing Matters

up his friends. "I am enjoying poor health, as servants say," he added, trying to make light of his appearance.

"And what are you doing in the City?" George asked.

"Oh, I am getting money to go to Switzerland. I am ordered there. I leave to-morrow—I did not want to bother you, old man. How is M—M—Mary?"

George told him of their great happiness. Guy listened listlessly, and excused his haste to catch the train at Cannon Street Station, which they had now reached.

The next day by the doctor's orders the invalid started for Pontresina. Guy took with him only an old servant with whom he shared the solitude of a little mountain chalet.

But the mountain air and all the snows were unavailing against the inward burning-up of the wanderer, and Guy slowly descended the Great Valley.

Meanwhile, Fate, having enmeshed one victim with its inexorable net, turned to weave its spell in the home of the Inglefields. The spring flowers were already the harbingers of what seemed to man's hope the flower of all the world, but the envious gods teach us to beware of sorrow when we are most happy. As the day of the supreme consummation of his love drew near, George

"The Evil That Men Do"

prayed that Heaven might bless him with a son. But He that giveth also taketh away.

On April 10th, Mary, the beloved wife of George Inglefield, gave birth to a son, and within a week the mother died.

Her husband's simple soul bore his great loss with humility, and Mary was buried in the little churchyard at Arlington, where lay the ancestors of the new-born heir to all the Inglefields.

As at the birth of the child, George's first thought was that his friend might share his great joy, so to Guy he first imparted his terrible loss. In reply to his brief message, George received from Guy a long, incoherent letter which seemed to betray a mental and physical collapse. George's grief touched a yet deeper abyss in the reflection that the two great passions that had informed his life should be engulfed in this sea of sorrow.

He remained at Arlington unable to tear himself away from the neighbourhood of her who had been the all in all of his manhood's love, until he felt his mind becoming distraught, and often he would sit by his wife's grave with her little baby in his arms.

He could not move away. He was benumbed with grief. From this state of torpor he was startled one morning on receiving a telegram

Nothing Matters

from Pontresina—not from Guy, but from his faithful servant. It ran thus:

Fear master dying. Too ill to travel home. Doctor advises nearest relations come here. Am telegraphing against Mr. Barrimore's wish, but felt it my duty to inform you.

George knew that this meant Guy's death. He at once gave orders to pack his trunk, and feeling secure as to his beloved child's health, he left it in charge of his mother and the nurse, and started for the Continent by the night train; nor did he stop his journey until he had reached Pontresina, whither he travelled by diligence from Khur. On his arrival he was met by the doctor, who imparted to him the news that his friend might not live through the night. A nurse and Guy's only sister had been constant in their attendance on him. The doctor informed George Inglefield that the news of his coming had been broken to Guy, and that since that time he had fallen into a delirious state, which they had tried to palliate by narcotics; he accompanied George to the little hut in which Guy had preferred to live rather than to occupy an apartment in the adjacent hotel.

In this hut Guy passed many months. When the news of Mary's death came he underwent a change—the restlessness of death was

"The Evil That Men Do"

upon him. He would start up in the night and take long, lonely walks in the mountains, returning in the early morning hours exhausted in body and mind. Thus he contracted a fever, and symptoms of pneumonia soon showed themselves. Then he took to his bed. From his window he would watch the sunset every evening, and as his eyes became familiar with the great mountain peaks, so his mind grew to look calmly towards the vaster mountains of eternity to which his soul would soon take flight.

Of Mary he thought often and with the kind tolerance of understanding. To her he gave a pity which he did not indulge himself. He hoped that she had learned to love George before she died. She, too, had paid with tears for that brief hour of bliss. She, too, had sown joy and reaped sorrow.

Nothing can avail against the irony of Fate. Our destiny may be determined by a butterfly.

There was a knock at Guy's door. When George entered the room, Guy, by a movement of his hand, dismissed the two women from his bedside and was alone with George. The dying man smiled feebly as tears trickled down his wan cheeks.

"You have come to see me off, George," he said with a little humorous smile. "Don't talk business. I have no occasion to make a will, but

Nothing Matters

to my creditors I bequeath my masterpieces." This he said with a characteristic wave of his hand towards a stack of papers that cumbered the floor.

George took his hand and tried to speak.

"You will soon be better," he said reassuringly.

Guy shook his head and smiled. Then he spoke:

"George, George, I am sorry about—*her*."

"Guy," said George, "Mary loved you too. When she was dying, in her delirium she called your name twice."

Guy lifted his eyes and gave a little cough. A tiny jet of blood trickled from his lips. George tenderly wiped the blood away; then Guy gave a moan and, turning his eyes towards the mountains, said: "George, George, everything matters!" He gave a hectic laugh that was half a sob, threw back his head, and passing his frail, withered fingers through his hair, he fell back with the look of a child upon his face. George held his hand and listened; the heavy breathing had ceased.

A tired fly settled on Guy's forehead—and another—and yet another. George knelt down by the bed and prayed for the soul of his dead friend.

CHAPTER VII

THE PITY OF IT

AND George buried Guy in the little churchyard at Arlington by the side of Mary, his wife. And he called the boy Guy, after him. And to his dead friend he raised a lasting monument.

Guy's posthumous fame was George's lifework, a labour of love which he divided with the care and education of his son, in whose young face, with a subtle melancholy joy, he saw his dead wife's beauty reflected, for the child was to him the image of its mother.

From the first all went well with the heir of the Inglefields. He passed from an unimperilled infancy into a vigorous childhood. Directly he was old enough to take notice of the world and life's vanities, he became the friend of his father, whose deep and passionate nature found expression in this devotion. They saw life with the understanding of contemporaries. Thus the father kept his youth, and thus the son was wise beyond his years. Young Guy at the age of twelve partook of his first lunch at the club with the ease of an old member. The boy betrayed in early youth that fondness for good food and good wine which distinguishes those who are gifted with a sensitive organisation. He who loves sonnets and sunsets appreciates good food and wine. An artist of my acquaintance makes a point of asking that he may be not only grateful for the feast, but that he may be given the grace to enjoy it with understanding.

The choice of a career was a frequent subject of discussion between these two, and though a journey on the Underground Railway had inspired Guy with leanings towards the engine-driver's lot, the sight of a *Britannia* boy at a children's party filled him with an unquenchable longing to become a midshipman and subsequently an admiral. Sir George Inglefield in no way opposed the boyish impulse, for he wisely doubted whether any public school education equalled the advantages of a cadetship in the national service for healthiness, discipline, and the development of independence of character and originality of mind. Even if the bent of young Guy's aspiration should later be on different lines, another career could be chosen, while he would have the experience of his early discipline as an asset. In due time Guy passed into the *Britannia*, went through his course with credit, blossomed into a full-blown midshipman, and was presently appointed in that capacity to one of the newest cruisers commissioned for a

The Pity of It

relief on the China Station. The prospect thus entailed of a long separation from his son acquainted George Inglefield with the first new sorrow he had felt since the loss of his wife and friend. But he bore up bravely; told the lad to keep his eyes open for Eastern wonders, and to write by every post; significantly hinted at a banquet worthy of Lucullus to celebrate his return home (for Guy was already an epicure), and with a tear in his eye and an ache in his throat watched H.M.S. *Ariadne* clear from Chatham one spring morning.

The father's last act was to thrust into the boy's hand an édition de luxe of Guy's aphorisms, entitled "Unworldly Wisdom." The preface set forth that the work had been "edited as a memento of a lifelong friendship by George Inglefield."

His separation from his son turned Inglefield's mind once more to the past, and to the literary labours of love which had occupied him contemporaneously with the boy's education. The tendrils of a vanished friendship clung closer about his heart; he recalled in many an hour of tender retrospection the Guy of the past, and he dwelt with a pardonable and unselfish pride on his own collations and editorial labours. "Thistledown from a Grave," consisting chiefly of love sonnets, went through twenty editions in as many months; a light-hearted series, entitled "Women Who Have Not Loved Me," had a brilliant sale;

Nothing Matters

while a more serious work, "The Ethics of Political Economy," is still a textbook of statesmanship. Guy had always been a rebel, and his work on "The Evolution of Socialism" has inspired minor thinkers of to-day with some of their most brilliant quotations; while the constructive genius of Mr. Bernard Shaw's political immortalisms has lately been declared to be but a "parodic echo of Guy Barrimore's 'Meditations in Westminster.'"

It is difficult to be wholly popular until one is quite dead, and criticism was almost unanimous in praising the posthumous works of Guy Barrimore. Those who would have made mouths at him while he lived, exhausted the vocabulary of praise when he was dead, although a satiric rhapsody, entitled "The Madonna of the Yellow Rose," written to the rhythm of a Hungarian *czardaseh*, and dated Rome, 1900, was pronounced to be a bitter indictment of the inconstancy of woman, somewhat out of harmony with the urbane spirit which animated the muse of this erratic poet, who, in his happier moods, made words into jewels and flung them at the moon.

The years rush by before we have time to count them; and after his long absence on service young Guy, now a lieutenant, was on his way home on leave from the China Station. For days Inglefield had been busying himself with pre-

The Pity of It

parations for this event. The chambers in St. James's Street were bright with decorations, and for the banquet a chef had been specially "retained." With a heart full of love and anticipation, the father started in the afternoon to meet the home-comer at Tilbury. So perfect a happiness had not possessed George Inglefield since his marriage morning; there was not a cloud on the broad firmament of his joy. As the train approached Tilbury he could hardly repress his exaltation. He greeted his boy, taking his head between his hands and kissing him in the old-fashioned way.

Young Guy had grown tall and straight, and George Inglefield rejoiced at the evident health of the youth, on whose tanned face there was not a trace of the troubled look he had noticed in the pictures of some of his ancestors.

The two sat down to dinner and talked of old times, Guy relating his experiences and discussing his future. He was profuse in his appreciation of the Lucullic feast provided, and both did ample justice to the wine that lifted them into the rarefied altitude where humour and sentiment blend. They were at the top of their being, seeing life as through a glass lightly.

The father lifted his glass and gaily pledged his son; Guy threw back his head and passed his hand through his curls.

George Inglefield's glass fell from his hand and

Nothing Matters

shivered on the floor. It was his dead friend sitting opposite him. In a lightning flash the panorama of events stood out as clearly before him as if they had been printed in black on a white page; he understood—he knew. He sank back in his chair, then gave a long indrawn moan that sounded like a great ship breaking on a rock, and without a word he staggered from the room in frenzy.

Events, incidents, rushed through his brain: Guy's estrangement — his wife's frequent apathy —her calling out Guy's name in her delirium—his pretended absence abroad—his lies on meeting —the drugs to numb consuming passion—his conscience-stricken look—his last words; the thousand little links connecting the great chain of catastrophe—all were realised with the exaggerated clearness of a madman's vision. Then came the sudden dread of insanity that had possessed him all his life. Yes, he was going mad—his friend, his wife: his noble soul could not conceive that it could be. Yes, madness had gripped him at last, he thought. He could not live with madness. He never stopped till he had reached the place where his wife and his friend lay side by side in the little churchyard at Arlington.

Now he too lies buried there.

*   *   *   *   *

The following extract from the report of the

The Pity of It

coroner's inquest completes this record of the life of George Inglefield:

    An inquest was held yesterday on the body of Sir George Inglefield, Bart., whose sad death has caused so great a shock throughout the country. The deceased baronet was found in the family cemetery with a bullet through his heart. The jury brought in a verdict of temporary insanity. In the course of the evidence it was shown that several members of the Inglefield family had met death at their own hands, and the eminent specialist, Sir James Raeburn, testified that the late baronet had more than once, in consulting him, expressed an apprehension lest a similar fate should befall him. The remains of Sir George Inglefield will, by request of his only son and heir, now Sir Guy Inglefield, be buried at Arlington.

    *   *   *   *   *

Nothing matters!
The pity of it:
Everything matters.

II
The Mystery of Howard Romaine

II
The Mystery of Howard Romaine

CHAPTER I

STRANGE DISAPPEARANCE OF A SUICIDE

NO *cause célèbre* of recent years has given rise to more futile speculations, more unsolved theories, than has the mystery of Howard Romaine. To those versed in the personal history of the stage the name of Howard Romaine is a household word; but for the sake of that larger public to whom the Romaine case is but as a half-forgotten nightmare it may be well to put on record the main facts of the case before I proceed to unravel the mystery in which this remarkable romance has hitherto been shrouded.

The following paragraph appeared in a late edition of an evening paper dated October 16th, 1887:

We regret to announce the sudden demise of Mr. Howard Romaine, a much esteemed actor. Our representative, having called to interview his bereaved

Nothing Matters

landlady, elicited the fact that Mr. Romaine was discovered in his sitting-room, fully dressed for the part of Hamlet, with one hand grasping a presentation copy of Shakespeare, the other a bottle labelled "Poison." Whether this untoward occurrence is to be traced to the hand of a murderer or a suicide is as yet an open question.

On the following morning, most of the newspapers contained obituary notices of the deceased, the cause of the startling occurrence was hotly discussed, and poor Romaine's posthumous praises we sung by many a voice. Yet, to tell the truth, Romaine was not a brilliant man; but partly from a feeling that no ill should be spoken of a man at his post-mortem, and partly perhaps from a sense of gratitude for the excellent copy he had been the means of supplying, Romaine's biographers dealt leniently with his memory. An elaborate and laudatory article, "By One Who Knew Him," appeared in the *Paddington Pioneer* of the following morning.

Mr. Howard Romaine occupied chambers in Clifford's Inn. The rooms, which consisted of a bed- and sitting-room communicating, were poorly furnished, the chief decoration being playbills, in which Romaine's name figured, and picture-posters, in which the deceased gentleman was represented in the act of rescuing maidens in distress, or hurling villains to their doom over yawning precipices.

Strange Disappearance of a Suicide

Beyond the fatal bottle labelled "Poison" there was little to supply a clue to the act of violence (self-inflicted or otherwise) to which Mr. Romaine had fallen a victim. The discovery of a pine-wood coffin, however—an article of furniture not usually found in a well-regulated household—pointed, in some minds, to the theory that the act had its origin in one of those temporary aberrations to which our more sensitive and highly-strung natures are prone. Pending the public inquiry, which was to take place on the following day, the body of the deceased actor was placed in the expectant coffin, and the door of the chambers was locked, barred, and carefully sealed on the outside. Public interest, which already ran high, was destined to receive a further shock by the startling news, announced in the evening paper, to the effect that Mr. Romaine's body had disappeared, and with it the now historical coffin.

CHAPTER II

THE MYSTERY DEEPENS

THE discovery of this cold-blooded and daring act, which stunned the public and paralysed Scotland Yard, distinctly pointed to the theory of foul play, and the question now arose, what motive could have actuated the body-snatcher in perpetrating this work of almost superhuman wickedness? Could the wild justice of revenge, conceived by the fathomless passion of a maniac, have urged him on to pursue his victim after death? Was it possible that an unhinged mind, wallowing in the refined brutality of Zolaistic crime, had sought to baffle justice by balking the verdict of a coroner's jury? asked the editor of an evening paper. Not the least astonishing phase of this outrage was its wanton boldness; for, it was argued, even if the body-snatcher succeeded in evading the vigilance of the porter on entering the lodge-gate, how could he have made his escape with the coffin and its load, unless, indeed, the porter himself were an accessory to the crime? This question was promptly answered by the arrest of the porter on suspicion, while a reward of

The Mystery Deepens

£500 was offered for any information which might lead to the discovery of the criminal at large. The remarkable fact that the seals on the door remained unbroken intensified the mystery surrounding the extraordinary case. Indeed, there were not wanting those who maintained that the body must have been spirited away by some occult force. A letter actually found its way into print supporting the theory that the removal might be the work of vampires—those intangible beings who, though scoffed at in an age of materialism and negation, have throughout history given intermittent evidences of their existence, and who belong to that unseen world to whose mystic manifestations the imaginative or soul-seers of all times have testified. Whichever theory may have been the true explanation of the fate which befell the departed actor, each was equally doomed to remain unsolved.

But little evidence of importance came to light during the searching investigation which immediately followed the discovery, resulting in a verdict against some person or persons unknown. It was shown that Mr. Romaine had led a sedentary life, that he avoided society, and that, having been out of an engagement for a considerable time, he had little or no personal property of value. The porter of the inn was the last to see Mr. Romaine alive. This functionary stated in evidence that

Nothing Matters

at about 5.30 P.M. on the evening of October 15th the unfortunate man passed through the lodge gate with the unmistakable intention of posting a letter, which he carried in his hand. Shortly after he re-entered the gate. His appearance was not more than usually gloomy.

One startling incident, however, which occurred during the ill-fated night threw a new and lurid light on the Romaine Mystery. At about 4 A.M. on the morning of October 16th a policeman named Hopkinson was found lying insensible on Waterloo Bridge. His helmet was broken as though crushed by some heavy weight. Hopkinson was at once removed to Charing Cross Hospital, where he lay in a critical state for some days. On recovering consciousness he made the extraordinary statement which filled the public mind with horror and indignation, and plunged the Romaine Mystery in still deeper and more hopeless darkness. In evidence, William Hopkinson, constable, deposed that on the morning of October 16th he was on duty in the Strand. The night was foggy. As Big Ben was striking a quarter to four, he saw a man hurrying along in the direction of Waterloo Bridge, staggering under the weight of what at first appeared to be a violoncello case, the property of a musician returning from a party, but which, on closer inspection, he discovered to be a coffin. The coffin-bearer was sobbing bit-

The Mystery Deepens

terly, and from humanitarian motives, which did even more credit to his heart than to his intelligence, the policeman refrained from questioning the mourner. In passing, the man, who wore a beard, had turned away his head, and therefore no description of his features by which the supposed murderer might be identified could be given. The policeman, however, watched the stranger till he reached the middle of the bridge, when by the fitful glare of a street lamp he saw him enter one of the recesses, bend over the coffin, and extract something from within. The policeman's curiosity being by this time awakened, he thought he would not be exceeding his duty in approaching the man, who appeared to be acting in so unusual a manner.

"What have you got in that there coffin?" he pertinently inquired. The man replied by seizing his load and running as fast as his feet would carry him, the policeman following. Seeing himself thus pursued, the criminal turned upon his opponent, and with one violent blow felled him to the ground, where he remained insensible. Hopkinson expressed a dim recollection of having seen the unknown individual mount the parapet with the coffin; he heard a fall, a splash below, but whether his assailant escaped, or hurled himself into the water, he was unable to state. The evidence proved beyond a doubt that the body-snatcher had, for some secret reason, cast

Nothing Matters

his victim into the river; but though fragments of the coffin and the Hamlet costume worn by the dead man were subsequently found floating towards Gravesend, although the resources of the Humane Society were taxed to the uttermost, although justice shrieked aloud to be avenged, no trace of Romaine's body would the sluggish waters yield, and no tittle of evidence has to this day been adduced to discover the identity of the murderer.

CHAPTER III

HIS OWN OBITUARY

TWO apparently disconnected incidents which had been overlooked by the police were the means of supplying the writer of the present narrative with the key to the mystery.

It will be remembered that, according to the evidence of the porter, Howard Romaine was seen to pass the lodge, with the apparent object of posting a letter, at the hour of 5.30 P.M. It will also be remembered that an elaborate obituary notice " By One Who Knew Him " appeared in the *Paddington Pioneer* of the following morning. This document, if sent by post, must have reached the printing office by the 9 P.M. delivery at latest, and was therefore posted before 6 P.M. Mr. Romaine's death could not, according to the evidence, have occurred before 7 o'clock. Accordingly, the article in question could only have been written by one (possibly the murderer himself) who had a foreknowledge of the impending catastrophe.

I was, for personal reasons, strangely interested in the fate of poor Romaine, and no sooner had

Nothing Matters

this startling conclusion entered my mind than I chartered a hansom cab, directing the driver to the address of the *Paddington Pioneer*. In answer to my anxious inquiries the editor informed me that the contribution in question was anonymous, that he was not acquainted with its author, but that he was evidently a sincere admirer of the deceased actor, as laudatory paragraphs concerning Romaine had frequently been contributed in the same handwriting. My surmise was confirmed —the letter *was* delivered by the last post on the night of October 15th. A strange suspicion began to shape itself in my brain. Pale with apprehension, I grasped the crumpled manuscript which was handed to me. One glance told me the horrible truth. My heart stood still, for the hand was the hand of my dead friend. Howard Romaine had written his own obituary!

CHAPTER IV

WHAT IS FAME?

I NOW pass from the historical aspect of the case to a brief survey of certain facts which have come to my knowledge, and in doing so I shall endeavour to lay bare the strange motives which led to the seemingly inexplicable catastrophe already described. How, when, and where this knowledge was obtained it is not for the reader to inquire, nor for the writer to obtrude. It may, however, be admitted that the information was imparted in a moment of extreme mental excitement and upon the most sacred promise that the incriminating statements should not be allowed to jeopardise the safety of their author. Should my statement be tinged with a partiality which the bare brutal recital of facts seems scarcely to justify, it should be borne in mind that the plea of extenuating circumstances may be claimed even for a body-snatcher, and that that same human weakness which urges men to commit atrocious crimes may also be the fountain of counter-balancing acts of a lovable nature; of these latter the present writer witnessed many instances at

Nothing Matters

the hands of an innocent because unconvicted criminal.

The student of human nature will not be surprised to hear that the crime which laid poor Romaine low was the offspring of Vanity—that prolific mother of the human passions. Vanity is the motive power of the world—for what is ambition but the vanity of the great? A man of considerable taste and learning, Howard Romaine was consumed by a morbid passion for notoriety, and having no other means of satisfying this craving, he gravitated towards the stage. He worked hard, he was conscientious, he was even enthusiastic, but he lacked originality—as an actor. He had studied for several years at a dramatic academy, he was an encyclopædia of dramatic lore, he could invariably tell the French source of an "original" English play, and he had a supreme reverence for the canons of Art; but he had no more personality than an Abernethy biscuit. He was one of the great All-Buts of life. He was, to speak the truth, a somewhat mediocre actor. Still, he was determined to shine in the dramatic firmament. How?—by acting? Yes. But to astonish the town, to shake artistic Europe to its foundations, it was necessary to cultivate notoriety. Howard Romaine had experienced that feeling of impotence, that sense of numbness, which comes to everyone who has tasted the bitter fruit

What Is Fame?

of unrequited ambition. But his was not a nature to be easily crushed—he would be great! He regarded the world as one great advertising hoarding. The fame of Howard Romaine should be on everybody's lips, his sayings should be quoted in the House of Commons, his doings should be recorded in the Sands of Time. His name should flare in letters of blood by day, should blaze in luminous paint by night.

The ingenuity with which he devised cunning schemes to dazzle the world was astounding. He raised advertising to a fine art. He cultivated a unique appearance; he wore strange and wonderful garments—his coat was the topic of the town, his hat was the pride of the Strand. As he passed people would stop in the street and inquire of the policeman on duty who was the extraordinary looking man. Then he would smile to himself and say: " They are beginning to talk about me." He made arrangements with enterprising tradesmen, and articles of wearing apparel were named after him—the Romaine hat, the Romaine tie, the Romaine umbrella, soon made their appearance. The comic papers made quips at his expense, and he exclaimed: " I have set the machinery of the Press in motion."

He gave banquets, he met with accidents and issued bulletins, he presented himself with testimonials, he published an autobiography, drove

Nothing Matters

his four-in-hand to the Derby, and almost succeeded in being familiar with Royalty. But public interest was on the wane, and "Jumbo" loomed on the horizon. So must ever the lion of the day make room for the elephant of to-morrow. Soon the houses were empty, and Romaine pined in thought. "There is something wrong with the public," he would say. Things went from bad to worse—he was on the brink of ruin. As a forlorn hope he determined to play *Othello*—it was his last throw of the dice. Never shall I forget that first night which proved the last. It was a disastrous—indeed, a historic—failure. So great was the fiasco that the house rose as one man, an incensed denizen of the gallery flung a ginger-beer bottle at our hero. Its aim was all too sure. As a friend of this remarkable man, I prefer to pass over the description of his great ignominy. Suffice it to say that on that memorable night poor Howard's nose was broken! So was his heart; his ambition was vanquished and, cursing fate, he retired into private life. Let us draw a veil over this interval of obscurity; in recording the event, even satire was dumb. Briefly, his occupation being gone, he for a time eked out a miserable existence, disdaining the food he could not afford to buy. At the point of the sword of hunger he consented to become a supernumerary in a pantomime, after proudly declining a sub-

What Is Fame?

scription set on foot by his former comrades, ever generous towards a vanquished rival.

It is sometimes misfortune which turns the tide of fate, and, in marring, makes us. Upon Howard Romaine the freak of fortune played a prank which made him all but immortal. Happy is the man who can make the silk purse of opportunity out of the sow's ear of misfortune. In spite of himself, Howard Romaine turned what was a visitation of providence into a gift of God.

Our hero's obscurity was short-lived, for having been appointed as understudy to one of the ugly sisters in the pantomime of Cinderella, he was called upon to undertake the part at short notice owing to a family bereavement of the leading low comedian. (It is extraordinary how frequent are funerals in the families of leading low comedians.)

The success of the understudy was immediate and phenomenal—the house rocked with laughter. Romaine's melancholy and, above all, his nasal twang, convulsed the audience. His surprise at the laughter he called forth, his pathetic indignation at his own triumph, evoked volleys of applause at the hands of a packed audience. As he himself observed in confidence to the writer: " In art, sir, it is easier to make the unskilful laugh by standing on one's head than to make the judicious weep by standing on one's feet ! "

Howard Romaine awoke the following morning

Nothing Matters

to find himself famous. " By request " he played the part every night; the evening papers contained leaderettes describing the delicate art of the new star; offers came by every post; and a famous author did homage to our popular hero by writing a comedy in which he shared the honours with a famous Society chiropodist who had lately figured in the Divorce Court, the title of the comedy being " She Stoops to Corncure: or, Is the Game Worth the Scandal ? " The production was an instant and overwhelming success; it would be difficult to decide whether the public was most attracted by Romaine's heaven-born affliction, by the scandal attaching to the lady's name, or by the author's wit.

Howard Romaine was the most talked-of man in London; he was asked to fashionable luncheons; within a short time he amassed a large fortune. I am bound to say that he was entirely unspoilt by fame. His manner to me in my early struggles always remained the same. He took his triumph with a shrug of the shoulders, and I remember that when complimenting him on his good fortune, he would cryptically reply, " Wait, laddie ! The day will come ! " This was the only comment he would vouchsafe to the present chronicler.

He had lived a simple life, in spite of his affluence. His eye was still on the tragic star.

One morning he called on a famous surgeon.

What Is Fame?

With that inimitable nasal accent which had made continents rock, and which potentates had vainly vied with each other to imitate, the world-renowned comedian thus addressed the man of medicine: " Cad you give be back by dose ? "

The operation on the broken member was duly performed, and Howard Romaine walked out of the consulting room a tragedian !

For a time he shrouded himself in mystery, wrapping his mantle about him and preparing for the great day.

After a lapse of a few weeks, an announcement appeared in the papers setting forth that Mr. Howard Romaine had "forsaken the primrose path of comedy, and would once more woo the tragic muse," that he had secured the National Theatre for a season, and would appear in a tragedy, specially written to exploit those talents which had been too long allowed to remain in twilight. He appeared, supported by columns of his own advertisements. But, alas! it must be recorded that the new departure was only a *succès d'estime*. The public palate had been vitiated by the vogue of comedy, the taste for which Romaine had himself created—he was overshadowed by his own fame!

But Howard was not to be easily thwarted by fate; he was a man of resource. New schemes were devised to whet the jaded appetites of the

Nothing Matters

many-headed—something startling was required. He bought a coffin, which proved an excellent advertising medium; he was photographed in it and, it was reported, slept in it. He threatened to retire from the stage; he horsewhipped a critic for having compared him unfavourably with David Garrick; he even became a platonic co-respondent in a divorce case, but broke down under cross-examination, and was compelled to leave the Court without a stain upon his character. This was the last straw.

Howard Romaine's Sedan was at hand. He played Hamlet—for one night only. This preyed upon his mind, and his body succumbed.

His funds were soon exhausted. One notoriety remained—the Bankruptcy Court. He went through it. But poverty proved a bad advertisement. His friends deserted him; worse, his enemies ceased to attack him. The Romaine hats wore out, the Romaine cigarettes fell into disrepute. Even the coffin had lost its glamour. The once magic name no longer glowed prismatically on the hoardings; it was no longer sounded by the clarion of fame, but muttered by the muffled drum of failure; the comic papers ceased their lampoons; the gaiety of a nation was almost eclipsed. That name, which was once the signal for thunders of applause, now only awakened a derisive snigger when introduced at the fag end

What Is Fame?

of a vaudeville ditty. Romaine's proud spirit was maddened. He called the world ungrateful, and lived in a garret. He scanned the newspapers in vain for some mention of his name; he listened at street corners to hear it spoken, but in vain. Goaded to desperation by this conspiracy of silence, he made a wild resolve, inspired by a stroke of genius. His name should not be forgotten; it should be lisped by babes and mumbled by old men; he would build for himself a niche in the eternal history of the stage; leading articles should be written recording his last act. Perish fame! Live notoriety! Banish Westminster! Welcome Madame Tussaud's! If not hewn in marble, then moulded in wax!

Here is the clue to the mystery. Howard Romaine resolved to commit suicide, or perish in the attempt!

CHAPTER V

HIS OWN BODY-SNATCHER

BUT Fate is often stronger than the will of man. Against its decree Howard Romaine was powerless. This unfortunate man was destined to failure, even in suicide. The self-administered dose of poison was just one grain short of fatal; his death was but a coma.

It was morning. Howard Romaine rubbed his eyes. His first feeling was one of oppression; his bed seemed too small; he moved; he felt himself hemmed in on all sides; he breathed; he tried to think. Dimly, through misty fumes of stale opium, he mused: "This, then, is the other world. How different from what I had pictured! How cold!" The woebegone little clock adorning the mantelpiece struck three times. Howard Romaine was recalled to life; he started up, but was repulsed by the coffin-lid. With one great effort he projected his whole strength against his wooden prison, and the lid flew open wide, letting in the morning air. Howard Romaine pressed his hands to his burning temples; reason was returning; memory swung open its gates. Suddenly the whole truth flashed

His Own Body-Snatcher

before him, as with one bound he reached the cold kamptulicon. Life had returned; a sudden storm shook his frame, an avalanche of emotion overcame him, and he fell sobbing on his bed. The clock struck the quarter; the man rose and struck a match. With a lighted candle he searched the room for the evidence of his crime—the bottle had disappeared!

His eye lighted on a paper in an unknown handwriting—he read the certificate of his own death. The horrible reality began to dawn on him—this certificate—that sheet; he had been placed in the coffin as a dead man! A revulsion of feeling had come over the would-be suicide, and shame for his folly mingled with his instinctive gratitude for life. To remain where he was was impossible; he must fly away and hide. A new energy seized him. Every moment was precious. He looked about for his portmanteau to pack a few necessaries; the rest of his belongings he could leave behind to pay his rent. Then he remembered that he had sold his portmanteau to pay a debt—there was no other box. The only receptacle within reach was the coffin. Hastily he packed two suits of clothes; then, struck with a sudden inspiration, he remembered his inky cloak and hose. These also he threw into the coffin. He dressed quickly, slipped a false beard hastily over his ears, and placed his hand upon the latch; the

Nothing Matters

door refused to yield to his pressure. He threw his whole weight against the oak, but without avail. The cold perspiration stood on his brow; like a rat in a cage, he ran backwards and forwards in despair. He peered through the open window —no escape—a smooth wall extended from the fifth floor to the ground. A smaller window opened on to the leads. Through this aperture he crept silently, in the hope of espying some friendly opening in the neighbouring house—a dead wall met his distracted gaze. Still he groped on—a heavy weight struck his forehead. Instinctively he grasped the object, which proved to be the chain suspended from a crane used in the building of an adjacent house. Help seemed to be at hand; but on closer examination Romaine discovered that a space of several feet yawned between the two buildings. To leap the intervening chasm was impossible. He crept back to his room, and taking the coffin on his shoulders, he once more regained the open air. Using the coffin as an improvised bridge, he crossed its creaking planks and gained the scaffolding of the next house. Saved—and by his own coffin! Quickly he seized the chain of the crane and slipped it round the ribs of the coffin, which now swung suspended over the depths beneath. Turning the wheel of the crane, he saw the coffin gradually disappear through the fog, till the slacken-

His Own Body-Snatcher

ing of the chain told him that the load had reached the ground. Then, seizing the chain between his hands and feet, he accomplished the perilous descent, and found himself in the open street. Once on firm ground he felt a new life vibrating within him, and as he made his way through the fog, the acts of his past life spread before his mind like a panorama. Drowning their folly in his tears, he muttered, "Posterity will never understand me."

The encounter with the policeman was accurately described in the evidence of the injured man. Goaded to desperation, and fearing the consequences that might ensue from his apprehension, the erstwhile actor defended himself with the only weapon at his disposal. The repentant suicide had become a murderer! Worse—he was his own body-snatcher!

CHAPTER VI

HUSH!

HOWARD ROMAINE stooped down; he saw the motionless face of his victim, he felt the hangman's rope around his neck, he saw the scaffold in his mind's eye, he heard the shouts of the applauding populace in his mind's ear, he even thought he detected a hiss, a sound to which he had of late become a stranger. The noise of approaching footsteps recalled him to his senses. His impulse to throw himself into the water below was checked by the conviction that he would again fail in his purpose, and he was not fit to die. He hurled the incriminating coffin over the parapet, and with the wings of despair fled from the spot. On, on, through the fog he ran, till he was lost in the hum of that vast ant-hill of humanity which swarms across the river.

My tale is told; my vow shall be kept. The veil of mystery must again be drawn round the sanctity of a private life.

We who, with a wink or a sigh, according to our respective points of view, have witnessed the spectacle of the dramatic Muse ravished by the

Hush!

advertising agent, must not judge harshly this amiable but too ambitious man, who possessed the warm heart and the ready sympathy which frequently characterise the egotist's nature. He had thought notoriety was everything. He was wrong. It is only 25 per cent.

* * * * * *

Have you, gentle reader, in your perambulations on the beach at Brighton, ever noticed a venerable old man, suspended from whose shoulders by two straps is a tray on which are exposed brandy-balls of singular transfulgence and luscious sweetness? When little children flock around him, he will pat their heads and exclaim with pointed finger: " Brandy-balls! They are better to-day than they were yesterday! "

As the south wind plays gently with his somewhat thin and straggly locks, he has the air of a man who, having experienced the buffets of life, has soared above their petty sway. A world-weary smile plays about his lips, suggesting a mild contempt for nigger-minstrels. His look is of one who feels himself unworthy to tie his own shoe-strings. Now and then he will be heard to mutter snatches from the immortal bard.

Can the reader guess his secret?

Hush!

III
The Stuffed Mouse

III

The Stuffed Mouse

MY friend, ——, is an oddity. He is of independent means, lives in chambers in the Albany, and is still a bachelor. I have it on his own authority that his life contains but one *grande passion*. I will endeavour to relate its final episode as briefly as possible.

It was after dinner. His room is filled with trophies and curios. My eye lighted on one object which occupied the place of honour on the mantelpiece. It was a stuffed mouse.

"What on earth," I asked, "makes you keep that stuffed mouse under a glass?"

"Ah!" he replied. "Thereby hangs a tale.'

"Unfold it to me," said I.

The hero of my story is a somewhat reserved man, but we were friends of many years, and Burgundy sets going the wireless telegraphy between heart and tongue. Besides, we had a common bond of sympathy in the mystery of one who is dead.

"You remember poor Dick Willoughby?"

Nothing Matters

"Yes," I murmured. "He died of drink, in Boulogne. There was something mysterious about him. He always had a haunted look. I hear he treated his wife shockingly."

"Y-e-e-s," replied my host. "So they say."

I had myself visited the Willoughbys during their early married life. I have never known a more remarkable woman than Dick's wife, nor have I ever seen a face more beautiful than hers. It was the face of a weeping Madonna; her eyes, when fixed at the approved artistic angle of forty-five degrees, would have melted the heart of the most hardened President of the Divorce Court. Her eyes were of a peculiar colour; they were like the sea playing over purple rocks. I saw them once shining through the darkness like dusky opals; when intent, they appeared to contract and dilate, like the eyes of a sacred sphinx in twilight. There was, indeed, a suggestion of the Eternal Feline about this wondrous creature. After her separation from poor Dick Willoughby she parted her hair in the middle, and wore a melancholy and almost sainted air, which was even more captivating than the lighter mood of her earlier happy days.

In parting from her husband she in no way lost caste; indeed, she was taken up by men and women of light and leading. Many were the stories of her platonic triumphs—her name was

The Stuffed Mouse

in turn coupled with those of some of the greatest in the land; indeed, a cynic said that she kissed her way through Society into the highest circles. But even the breath of scandal could not displace the invisible halo which hovered over the fair brow of the weeping Madonna of the upturned eyes. One of her peculiar fascinations when engaged in conversation was the impression she gave of saying with her eyes, "This is the moment of my life; I have not lived in vain." I have watched her with this look on her face subjugating six different men on one and the same evening. I believe it was genuine—some women have this supreme genius—the sincerity of the moment. These thoughts I imparted to my friend as we drank our coffee.

"Poor Dick!" I went on. "I could never understand why, in all his ravings, he never mentioned her name. I imagine he died of remorse."

"Perhaps," rejoined my host. "Or was it a broken heart?"

We puffed our cigars in silence. My friend looked at me.

"I loved her, too," he said quietly. "Let me tell you the story of the stuffed mouse."

I listened.

"I loved her for years, and I never told my love to her. I have never told it to anyone till

Nothing Matters

now. You shall be my father confessor. All the years I knew her while she was Willoughby's wife, I pitied her. I even had a row with Dick about his treatment of her. He never said a word. When he died I brought her the news. She was too overcome to order her mourning. I undertook this delicate commission. I loved her secretly for years. I took my secret to the war with me. I thought of her night and day, and I wrote to her once a month. When I returned home I hardly dared to see her—she was too sacred to approach. I knew that I could not keep my secret pent up longer, and dreaded the terror of her indifference. I, who had gone through many a fight without dread of death, was a poltroon in love. The more one cares, the less one dares. For two whole days I hesitated. Then I wrote a little note:

" ' Could she see me alone—and when ? '

" ' Come this afternoon ; I have been lonely,' was the reply.

" My mind was made up. That very afternoon I would ask her to be my wife. I had bought my courage with my despair. She was sitting in her room in her tea-gown, her hair was tumbled over her shoulders. A white cat was curled in her lap, a little silver bell was suspended from its neck.

" ' Bring in the tea,' she said to the servant

The Stuffed Mouse

maid; and we sat down. For a time we talked of the world, but each seemed to feel the world was a thing remote. There was a long silence. A little sigh escaped her lips. There was another silence, and I echoed the sigh. My hand touched hers; my fate and hers were one. The great moment of my life was at hand.

" ' Will you,' I said with trembling lips, ' will you—— ? '

" At this moment a strange sound interrupted the completion of the sentence. The silver bell tinkled. Our eyes turned. We saw a little mouse which the cat had sprung upon, and was torturing with its claws, in pleasant dalliance. I heard the tiny squeak of the tortured animal.

" ' Let me save that mouse ! ' I cried. ' I can't bear to see its agonies,' and at once I made to snatch it. The ' Madonna ' grasped my arm and pulled me on to the sofa by her side.

" ' No,' she said in a whisper. ' Let us watch them.'

" I sat with open mouth, gazing at the woman's face. Her opalescent eyes were contracting and dilating. A look of intense pleasure darted from them. Once more the cat tossed its prey into the air, and the little animal lay in the convulsions of death. I saw a strange, hunted look on its face. Where had I seen that look before ? It was the look in poor Dick Willoughby's eyes.

Nothing Matters

" There was a long silence. Once more the cat was purring in her mistress's lap. With her eyes at the angle of forty-five degrees, the love of my life turned to me smiling:

" ' Now, tell me, what is it, dear one ? '

" I paused. Then she continued :

" ' You were saying, " Will you—— " Will you what ? '

" A new courage was with me as I replied :

" ' Will you—give me another cup of tea ? ' "

* * * * * *

I looked at my friend, and he looked at me.

" That's all," he said. " Now you know why I stuffed that mouse ! "

IV
The Stout Gentleman

IV

The Stout Gentleman

IT is long past midnight as I sit, my eager pencil in my hand, waiting for an inspiration for my story. But the fount of my imagination is dry. My brain is as sluggish as is that of the November fly as it wends its paralytic way across the blank sheet of paper that lies in front of me.

I look up. On the wall opposite me hangs the copy of a famous picture by Velasquez—that of a mediæval *bon vivant* whose character has not been unfolded, whose life has not been vouchsafed to the world save on the canvas of the great Spanish painter. I had often wondered what was the inner being, what were the emotions, the passions, the dark crimes of the Stout Gentleman whom the genius of Velasquez has actualised for us as vividly as Rembrandt has immortalised the carcass of a slaughtered beast in his famous work in the Louvre. How often had I gazed on that face of callous wit, of stolid indifference to human suffering! The history of the Inquisition was summed up in the mighty

Nothing Matters

visage of that "boulting hutch of beastliness" —a face as cruel as the world's east wind, as cold as criticism, as relentless as that of the forbidding God of one's frenzied childhood.

My eye becomes transfixed as I wonder and gaze, and gaze and wonder. Suddenly the broad countenance and the bulky form seem to step from the frame, and the secret told in the picture is revealed to me as by hypnotic suggestion. I give it to the world:

The Stout Gentleman lived in a lonely castle in the mountains of Fea.

The castle could be approached only by a drawbridge on the one side, while it was inaccessible on the other side, which was situated on a sheer cliff descending five hundred feet. There were reasons why the abode of this great noble should be immune from intruders, for many an ugly tale was told on the countryside of dark deeds done by the tyrant; there were many fathers and brothers whose hands went to their daggers at the mention of his name.

If one scrutinises the picture with a magnifying glass, one can detect the suggestion of a mail shirt nestling round the fat neck of the grandee, into whose family history I do not propose to enter in this brief record of the incident which Velasquez has seized in his picture, beyond recording the fact that his unhappy wife had died

The Stout Gentleman

mysteriously. It was whispered that she had had a clandestine love affair with a nameless fair-haired Englishman, and it was reported that he had fallen at the sword-point of the Stout Gentleman, who devoted his life to heartless pleasure, who regarded women as the slaves of his passion, and whose chief interest in life centred in the pleasures of the table.

By some secret agency, everyone who opposed him ceased to be. It is recorded of him that he said in an expansive moment:

"Thank God, I have no enemies." And then added, with a strange smile, "They are all dead."

To the philosophy of food he dedicated his life. To the hunger of others he gave no thought. For him there was but one man—himself. There was but one God—*Himself*. Glance at his picture; the lines of self-indulgence are written there more clearly than can be described in inexpressive type. The Stout Gentleman made a point of ordering his meals himself, down to the smallest detail. Glancing at the landscape, he would often ponder over the bill of his fare for an hour at a time; his splendid digestion was the father of an abnormally healthy conscience; no qualms disturbed his gastronomy or his rest. He slept the deep sleep of the unjust.

Of his meals he was the sole partaker, save on the rare occasions when he entertained officially

Nothing Matters

in a manner that beggared Nero and bourgeoised Caligula. Convivial as he appeared to all who met him, he was yet a man who by choice ate and drank alone. He would invariably linger for an hour and a half over his repast, eating and drinking thoughtfully. He was good company to himself. Of him it was recorded by his body servant that he would often stop between the courses and laugh a loud laugh at his own thoughts, sometimes pausing to torture a parrot who was the sole co-occupant of the room. From long association and community of interests (the parrot was a huge feeder), a strange resemblance had grown between the man and the bird. To this parrot the Stout Gentleman would confide the blasphemous sallies of his wit, and when he laughed his deep, guttural laugh the parrot joined in, until their cachinnant vibrations caused the delicate glasses on the table to shiver in sympathetic pain, and to join in a humming accompaniment, like the ghosts of little children singing *à bouche fermée*. At this effect the gentleman in black was mightily pleased, and through the open window the echoing mountains swelled the pandemonic chorus of laughter.

It was time to order his supper; the Stout Gentleman summoned his head cook.

"Let it be a meal of simple splendour to-night," said the epicure thoughtfully, sucking the wind

The Stout Gentleman

from a hollow tooth. "A quail pasty done in the Andalusian manner — twenty quails, each stuffed with a truffle and three olives touched with garlic; this to be followed by a dish of stewed prunes."

Two flasks of the best wines his wide vineyards could afford, mellowed by many years, completed the ambition of the night. These instructions were conveyed through the parrot, to whom the Stout Gentleman always addressed himself in ordering his repast, as he disliked direct communion with his fellow-men.

The cook bowed to the parrot and went about his business. There was a knock at the door. A letter was handed in. The Stout Gentleman broke the seal.

"From Juan," he murmured.

Juan was his son, who asked permission to see his father, having travelled on horseback to the castle.

"Well, Juan," said the father, having bade him enter and extending his hand for the son to kiss. But he, a fair-haired youth, made no advance. He stood with his hands behind his back, and motioned with his head to the servant to leave the room. The Stout Gentleman hummed a gay tune, thrumming with big fat fingers on the table.

"Where is she?" the boy cried in concen-

Nothing Matters

trated passion, still holding his hands behind his back, lest they should close round the giant's throat in a patricidal grip.

"She? There are many shes in the world," retorted the Stout Gentleman. "But life is full of coincidences."

"She—Isabella. . . ."

There was a long pause as the father and son gazed into each other's eyes; the Stout Gentleman could hear the son's heart beating. Then he said slowly:

"So you are my rival! It was you who cut the traces and caused my horses to stampede over the precipice? The best pair of horses from my stables. His Holiness the Pope sent them to me."

"Where is she?" thundered the boy, springing like a wild beast on the giant.

"Wait!" said the Stout Gentleman, as he waved the boy to a convenient distance.

It was the old, old story of the love of an honest boy for a virtuous girl; of a sinister pursuit by a feudal lord; of the *droit de seigneur*; of proud defiance and contempt on the part of the maid; of the spiriting away of the victim after the convenient removal of the father. The agents of the Inquisition could tell many a tale of the kind in which the bravo plied his trade. Of the father of Isabella it is known that he was

The Stout Gentleman

detained by order of the Inquisition, and records show that various attempts were made to secure his escape; but whether any of these proved successful, or whether his name ever figured among those who suffered the *auto-da-fé,* I have been unable to ascertain.

In a torrent of frenzied eloquence the boy flung in the libertine's face his awful indictment, told of his discovery and of Isabella, from whose lips he had learnt the terrible truth: how she was again snatched from him, and of his solemn vow to kill the monster who had sought to desecrate the virgin shrine of his love.

The grandee sat immovable, replying only with a heave of his huge shoulders. There was another silence. Juan's gaze lighted on a miniature of his mother which hung upon the wall. His eyes were fixed on her delicate, dark face for many minutes. Then he spoke:

"Father, I despise you so deeply that I hope in giving life to me my mother sinned!"

The two men looked into each other's eyes in a recognising and realising stare. Opposite the grandee sat his deadliest enemy, who had died many a year ago. He was an Englishman who had fought against the Spaniards in the year 1620.

"Bastard!" muttered the Stout Gentleman between his teeth.

Nothing Matters

"One of us must die," said the boy.

"Yes," ruminated the Stout Gentleman. "Another enemy lives!"

In a moment two swords flashed and clashed in quick lightning play. Each impulsive thrust of the younger was parried with masterly agility by the elder man. The Stout Gentleman had long been renowned as the greatest swordsman in Castile. With his quick thought he had weighed the consequences of the death of Juan—it would be undesirable that he should kill his heir with his own hand. His attitude was merely one of defence. He was calmly reserving another fate for the successor to his vast estates; he would disinherit him by a death more terrible and less inconvenient than that of the sword. He took care that no thrust should cause an incriminating scratch on his own skin or on that of his adversary. The duel continued with increasing violence and recklessness on the part of the boy, and unabated coolness on the part of the other. The terror of that half-hour was increased by the horrible squawks and laughter of the blaspheming parrot.

"One of us must die," the boy panted hoarsely.

"One of us must kill himself," said the Stout Gentleman. "Let us talk. One of us must disappear. After all, it seems more becoming. For you to be a patricide would give you a bad name

The Stout Gentleman

—for me to be a filicide would not add to my popularity. Let us appeal to the judgment of the dice!"

"Give me the dice," said the boy.

They threw—the boy a double-six. It was the turn of his adversary.

"Three," cried the Stout Gentleman. "My lucky number."

Both men sat down at the table—the elder in deep thought.

"What are you thinking of?" asked the boy.

"Of my codicil?"

"Of my disinheritance?"

"No; of the confession of my sins."

A terrible gleam lit up the yellow eye of the Stout Gentleman as he took the pen.

"Write!" said the boy.

"Stop!" whispered the other. "I hear a noise of someone approaching the loggia. No one must know." He went towards the door and listened. "Write while I watch," he said.

The boy took the pen as the other dictated.

"I am leaving this world because I am unworthy to remain in it. Those I have wronged will, I hope, pardon me. Let masses be said for my soul in the Cathedral of San Sebastiano."

The man in black made a gesture that all was safe, and the other handed him the paper.

"Sign it!" said the boy.

Nothing Matters

"Why is the moon so red to-night?" asked the Stout Gentleman, pointing westwards to the mountain peaks.

The boy turned to look. With a mighty lurch of his huge shoulders the other thrust the boy through the open window. In falling over the parapet, to save himself Juan caught at the murderer's sword-belt. It escaped his grasp, but the buckle must have scratched him, for a little spurt of blood appeared on the hand of the gentleman in black.

Looking over the parapet to watch the descent, he exclaimed, "My last enemy!" Then he turned back to the table and glanced at the document written in the boy's own hand. "*His* confession," he said, allowing it to drop on the table. He noticed that two chairs were overturned. These he carefully put in their places; then he surveyed the room to satisfy himself that there was no sign of a scuffle.

The vesper bell in the neighbouring chapel told the Stout Gentleman the hour of his supper was at hand. A hunger came upon him as his dilated nostrils sniffed the scent of the cooking. He passed along the loggia towards the banqueting hall. There was a slight muffled sound. He turned to listen. (How wonderfully Velasquez has caught the moment!) It was only the rustle of a vulture's wing swooping valleywards.

The Stout Gentleman

"And now," said the Stout Gentleman, cautiously licking from his hand the tell-tale spot of the dead boy's blood, "and now for the quail pasty!"

* * * * * *

This is the end of my story, for, to my intense relief, the picture of the Stout Gentleman has moved back into its frame.

V

The Lament of a Lilliputian Twin

A FANTASY

V

The Lament of a Lilliputian Twin

A FANTASY

I AM a freak of Nature. I am one of two, or two of one. I am, in short, a semi-detached twin. We (how hateful to me is our plurality!) are known to fame as "The Royal Lilliputian Twins." By all civilisation we are recognised as the champions of the twin world, while from the Crowned Heads of Europe we have received the homage due to the phenomenal condition by which Nature has singled—or rather doubled—us out for distinction among our fellow-men. It is in no spirit of idle boast that I claim at least an equal share of that Divine Right which is conferred by kings upon themselves; for it is, after all, more difficult to be a twin with four legs and two heads, than it is to be a king with one head and two legs. Indeed, it is my opinion that there would be lacking in my dual state no element of superiority over the rest of mankind, were it not for the fact that my other half is an utterly contemptible,

Nothing Matters

not to say loathsome, being. While I am sympathetic, high-minded, proud, but of delicate physique, my brother is unintelligent, coarse, cunning, and self-indulgent, but robust. We have two brains, but one stomach. Imagine the horror of sharing a stomach with a man one despises! I am called Ham; my brother is known as Abra. We were christened Abraham; but, characteristically, my brother has usurped the first two syllables, leaving to me the Ham, the smaller share of our joint name.

I cannot disguise from myself that it is I who monopolise all the intellectual attributes of our dual nature, which by some subtle process I sap from my brother's mental being; he, on the other hand, absorbs my material being, and in a grovelling way exults over his superior physique. While my sensitive palate yearns for the delicate *pâté de foie gras*, my brother brutally battens on beefsteaks. Our minds diverge on every conceivable subject; in politics we have not a single idea in common, nor do our pleasures run in the same groove. He, being a low-minded person, constantly drags me to music-hall entertainments, where I read the *Quarterly Review* in sullen protest. On such occasions as I am permitted to indulge my taste for the music of the future at Philharmonic Concerts, the plaintive melody of the flute, the passionate vibration of

The Lament of a Lilliputian Twin

the violin, the matronly yearning of the violoncello are stifled by the sonorous snore of my inferior half. He gravitates towards the society of the betting-ring, while I incline to that of the scientific world, with whom my lot has often brought me in contact, and with whom it has frequently pleased me to discuss the strange phenomena of creation which have at various periods given to the world a Napoleon or a Hercules, a William the Conqueror or a Lilliputian Twin. There is, I positively believe, no limit to the achievements with which I, in common with these other abnormal specimens of humanity, might have startled the world, but for the dragging about with me of an entirely unsympathetic, not to say unpresentable, *alter ego*, from whose compromising companionship it has been impossible to free myself. Often in the dead of night, when reason has been clouded by sleep, have I, half-dreaming, thought to steal away; but ever has the stertorous snore of my portly brother recalled me to my double state, and reminded me that matter is stranger than mind!

How often have I not endeavoured to impress upon Abra that we owe it to the dignity of our privileged condition to dress in a becoming fashion! But here again we were entirely at odds, for while I, in common with royalty, prefer the incognito of a gentleman's walking dress, Abra will insist

Nothing Matters

on wearing the gala costume of a Red Indian chief. In consequence of this singular instance of bad taste, I found it necessary to cut my brother, and for an entire fortnight we were not on speaking terms.

It is with pain that I record another event which was productive of strained relations between us. The source of irritation was the divergence in our tastes in regard to the choice of society. Never shall I forget the occasion when, having enjoined Abra to be on his best behaviour, I had invited the most distinguished of modern professors to meet an eminent ecclesiastic at a recherché dinner. It had been my intention, through the means of good fellowship, to bridge over certain differences of opinion which are understood to exist on certain subjects between these two great men, and by a judicious blending of ideas to render science more orthodox and theology more scientific. That this consummation was destined to be frustrated I realised by the horrible discovery that Abra had seized the occasion to invite as his guests a well-known prize-fighter of notoriously intemperate habits, and a bookmaker whose morals were as questionable as his methods of expressing them.

To postpone the meeting was impossible. With an apology for the somewhat discordant element, whose presence I attributed to my

The Lament of a Lilliputian Twin

brother's eccentricity rather than to a lack of knowledge of the world, and with a graceful allusion on the part of the prelate to the merging of classes which our latter-day civilisation had effected, our dinner began most auspiciously. A complimentary reference on the part of the archbishop to our interesting dual state led me to unfold to my learned and reverend guests a theory on the origin of species, in which they both exhibited the liveliest interest. In their primitive condition, I contended, man and woman were permanently attached to each other. In this ideal social condition happiness was a natural law. Man and wife walked about the world in harmony: there was perfect love and accord between those so joined together; there was no inclination (leaving the physical impossibility out of the question) to stray from his or her natural mate: jealousy was unknown; the Divorce Court necessarily non-existent. The comparatively futile expedient of the marriage contract which has since been introduced can never compensate for the loss of this natural tie. A light at once consistent with science and with tradition is thus thrown on the all-important rib theory with which the scientific and theological worlds have been battling for centuries. Our earliest ancestors were undoubtedly attached to each other by a rib; but, owing to circumstances

Nothing Matters

into which it would be unbecoming in a mere layman to enter, poor humanity has lost its other half, and in the great blind man's buff of life is doomed to wander about the world in search of its natural mate—too often, alas! in vain. This is no idle theory, though it has hitherto not received its due recognition from a race puffed up with the conceit of its own single condition, which refuses to recognise the more ideal state from which it emerged.

At this point our symposium was rudely disturbed by a somewhat heated discussion between the pugilist and the bookmaker on the relative merits of "four-ale" and "half-and-half," of which these robust skeletons at the feast were respectively partaking. The professor, who was at this moment toying with a glass of Château Lafite, affected a courteous interest in these beverages, and, with that ease which is characteristic of good breeding, even ventured on a scientific, though brief, investigation of the proffered tankards. After this incident I observed a marked coolness between the prelate and the bookmaker, whose alluring overtures to play the confidence trick with the dignitary of the Church were met by a polite but firm evasion of this proposed test of friendship.

It was not, however, until dessert was in progress that the unseemly conduct of Abra and

The Lament of a Lilliputian Twin

his boon companions asserted itself, when the professor (whose exemplary conduct on this occasion I cannot too highly commend) was endeavouring to explain to the pugilist the descent of man, and in the most delicate way hinted at his distant ancestry. The prize-fighter, whose ruling passion was strong in drink, regarded this scientific allusion to his remote origin as a personal affront, and insisted on having a stand-up fight with the man of learning; while the blear-eyed bookmaker, now hopelessly intoxicated, shouted in a hoarse and strident voice the odds which he was prepared to lay on his professional friend. It was at this juncture that the archbishop left the table. Abra was by this time, I grieve to state, speechless with drink. My apologies for this gross lack of breeding on my brother's part were stifled in the general din of a scene from the description of which my pen shrinks. Suffice it to say that the meeting broke up in uproar and that the professor and I no longer recognise one another in the street.

Never shall I forget the occasion when my drunken brother Abra was summoned for assault and battery. Whilst he, after a severe censure from the bench, was being removed to the cells, I had the satisfaction of being assured by the magistrate that I left the court without a stain upon my character!

Nothing Matters

But it is in the more solemn questions of the heart that I have suffered the greatest indignities at my brother's hands. At a "Grand Combination Show of Nature's Royal Monstrosities" (so our American manager styled the entertainment which brought together the brightest talent of the phenomenal world), Fate threw in our path our female counterparts, the Two-headed Nightingale. I at once fell a victim to the charms of Miss Christine. We loved each other with a passion which is not given to human beings cast in the conventional mould; but, oh miserable lot! she too grew on the left side, so that when, mad with admiration, I rushed to embrace the object of my affections, I found that my hated brother stood opposite her, while I encountered her wholly unattractive sister. This was a terrible blow. The first flush of our budding love was blighted by the ever-hateful presence of one who, in the affairs of love, is incapable of soaring above the vain inanities of the fat lady attached to our show; and to whisper soft nothings across our other halves was out of the question. No hero of romance was ever placed in so pathetic, not to say invidious, a position as I. We (Miss Christine and I) cursed our fate. She, too, has a supreme contempt for her companion; she, too, cherishes aspirations towards higher things. For us the

The Lament of a Lilliputian Twin

world was out of joint. I will confess that I cursed my brother Abra. Nothing daunted, I declared my love to Miss Christine; but she, proud girl, jilted me on account of my "disreputable connections," for on the very day of our proposed wedding I was recovering from my brother's drunken debauch. Never would my betrothed consent to share the same roof with one who showed so little regard for the usages of society. Christine was always a lady.

What revenge could I devise? To challenge my brother to a meeting on the Belgian frontier was my first impulse. But, I reflected, if I killed Abra, his death would of necessity be followed by my own. In my despair I determined to commit suicide; but again I reflected that by this step I should be guilty of my brother's murder. Oh, miserable lot! Oh, futility of fate! Oh, luckless perfection! I am, and shall always remain, a broken-hearted bachelor. Let my lot at least serve as a lesson to mankind. Oh, my brothers, be reconciled to your inferiority! Rail not at being gifted with a short allowance of arms and legs. Remember that in an imperfect world ordinary beings possess advantages which go a long way to compensate for the physical inferiority of their condition. In this world, imperfection has its triumphs! The record of my unhappy fate teaches us that the innocent too often suffer

Nothing Matters

for the wicked, the weak for the vices of the strong. So too have I, the weaker vessel, invariably suffered for my brother's drunken bouts. His were the excesses; mine the delirium tremens. Even so have my tears ever fallen for his crimes.

"Two heads," the proverb says, "are better than one." But my story proves that, for the purposes of love, at least, this is a misleading fallacy.

HAM.

VI

The Ultimatum, or Every Man has his Price

VI

The Ultimatum, or Every Man has his Price

Characters: The RULER OF A GREAT PEOPLE; *a* CHIROPODIST; *Princes, Grand Dukes, Ministers of State, Priest, Professor, and Sycophants.*

Scene: The RULER'S *marble bathroom in the Palace.*
[*At the rise of curtain the* RULER OF A GREAT PEOPLE *is discovered seated in his dressing-gown; the* CHIROPODIST *plies his trade.*]

CHIROPODIST: What remarkable corns your Majesty has!

RULER: Yes, they are ancestral; all my predecessors were noted for them.

CHIROPODIST: I have heard, your Majesty, that in the seventeenth century many of the Court wore tight shoes in order to cultivate the Royal infirmity—[*correcting himself*]—prerogative!

RULER: I dare say. Take care—you hurt me. [CHIROPODIST *takes from his tray some drops from a little bottle labelled "Poison," applies them with a brush to the Royal foot, and resumes his pedicure.*] You may continue to address us.

Nothing Matters

CHIROPODIST [*after a pause, choosing his topic*]: The weather, your Majesty, is very—very regrettable.

RULER [*with the Divine-right manner*]: Yes, we are much displeased with the weather!

CHIROPODIST: Yet the peasants have prayed for fine weather for the occasion of your Majesty's name-day.

RULER: The prayers of peasants are not always heard. To-day is Friday, is it not? I have a superstition against signing important documents on Friday. To-night it is the Ultimatum. [*Bored.*] Oh, this war! What is the feeling among the people? You have leave to speak the truth.

CHIROPODIST: Your Majesty is too gracious. The people, your Majesty, do not wish for war.

RULER: The Minister of War assures me they do.

CHIROPODIST: The people, your Majesty, will regard the decision of their King as the will of God. [*Bowing over the Royal foot.*]

RULER: You are a clever fellow. You might go far.

CHIROPODIST [*with momentary expansion*]: My hump has stood in my light, your Majesty.

RULER: There is a saying of my great ancestor, "It is lucky to have a hunchback near you."

CHIROPODIST: Yes, your Majesty, the common proverb says, "A hump is a misery to him who

The Ultimatum

hath it, but fills him of the straight back with contentment."

RULER: We all have our compensations.

CHIROPODIST: Yes, your Majesty, my mother always had a premonition that before I died a great honour would be conferred on me.

RULER: I shouldn't wonder. By the by, I should like to keep you near me to-night. Your hump may bring me luck. I have to make a momentous decision. Now listen to me. I trust you—you have availed yourself of my permission to be truthful. I do not trust all my servants. Will you look to the wine to-night? [*The* CHIROPODIST *cringes assent.*] The Royal Dukes and my Ministers are to dine at my table. Be near me to-night, my little hunchback.

> [*The* CHIROPODIST *kisses the Royal toes in deep obeisance. The* RULER OF A GREAT PEOPLE *exits to his dressing-room. The* CHIROPODIST *rises.*]

CHIROPODIST: It has come—the day, their day, my day! God of my fathers, keep me from madness. Mother, hold my hand from out of your grave! You said it should be! My hunger can be stilled—I can almost straighten my back with pride. [*He crosses himself beneath the image of the Virgin.*] Help me in my hour. There are two roads—which shall I take? I have learned to flatter—it is my profession. I have walked

Nothing Matters

across the plank—I am there; my ambition, my little ambition, can be requited. I have blackmailed the world—I am in its palace. The open road is in front of me at last. I can move step by step, as others have done, nearer the throne—and then, who knows? But there is another road—the road where humanity toils and trudges; the road my father and mother trod when I was a little child. It was the revolution; my mother was torn from my father's arms; before his eyes she was degraded by the soldiery—then they shot him for an anarchist. This hump of mine—a soldier struck me with his gun—my shoulder shattered. In our exile every night my mother would stroke my back while she prayed that God would straighten me. She starved that she might sprinkle my hump with holy water. And here I am what I am. This is my moment—shall I fall to ease, to comfort, and convenience? I whose father shrieked for freedom as he fell. This war—I can prevent it. I see it coming on. I am not blind as those that make war—war for the vanity of a King. War for greed of commerce. Hundreds, thousands, millions of lives will be lost to satisfy the lust of five men! Can five hundred years of happiness compensate for one year's spoil of a monarch's sport? An Emperor of the Shambles declares war to make a madman's holiday. I can hear the yells of the

The Ultimatum

poor deluded men in the trenches—they call it glory! I can see their stark bodies mangled and twisted in the frozen mud—they call it glory! I can smell the stench of their decay wafting disease through the land in the spring that is coming—they call it glory! I can read the outpourings of their hireling professors. I hear Christ's priests chanting their blessings on the holocausts—they call it glory! The moans of millions of mothers go up to God, unheeded by man. My mind is a mirage of ruined cathedrals, of devastated homes, of spectres of famished peoples—all these I see—they call it glory! My little hand can stay all this. [*He takes from his box the little bottle labelled " Poison."*] Here is my ally—a few drops of this in his liqueur to-night, and it is done. [*He tastes the poison.*] Revenge is sweet! I shall be the undying benefactor of mankind. After all, he is only one man, like myself. He who cuts the corns of a monarch knows the equality of man. Murder—yes. To kill one man is to be a murderer; to kill ten thousand is to be a hero! Strange is the logic of the world! What is he, then, who murders one to save millions? [*He takes up his paraphernalia and exits.*]

> [*The scene changes to the private dining-room of the great* RULER. *Seated round the table are Princes, Cabinet Ministers, a* **Professor**,

Nothing Matters

and a Priest. It is the end of dinner. There are signs of debauchery. The RULER, *steeped in wine, gazes before him with pale eyes. Papers are in front of him and an inkstand, into which he dips his pen irresolutely. The clock strikes twelve.*]

WAR MINISTER: At twelve the decision was to be given; it has already struck.

A PRINCE: Octavian, sign.

[*The* RULER *hesitates and takes a liqueur from the hands of the now resplendent* CHIROPODIST.]

PRIME MINISTER: It is time to sign, your Majesty.

RULER: I am thinking.

PRIME MINISTER: A King should never think, your Majesty, when he knows his power. It is two minutes past the hour—history is rushing by. You are two minutes less powerful than you were at midnight.

WAR MINISTER: Might is right.

RULER: Is Might always right? [*Turning to elderly Priest.*] Father, you have often told me that the true divine right of kings is peace. What did you say in your sermon during the Peace Conference? If the sacred head of the State were to pronounce himself to the world as the leader of Peace—if he will declare himself—if he will proclaim that the highest prerogative of kings, their true divine right is universal peace

The Ultimatum

—if in his greatness he will carry this ideal into effect, then he will go down the centuries not only as King of his land, not only as Emperor of the globe, but as the temporal saviour of mankind. Those were your words, father. Surely God is good.

PRIEST: Yes, your Majesty, very good. But now we are talking war. The needs of your people sanctify the sacrifice of your ideals.

RULER: I am wondering at what point a King is justified for the sake of his country in sacrificing his ideals. [*He takes another liqueur.*]

PRIEST: His conscience must decide.

PROFESSOR: Ideals are only official ideals when they have concrete foundations. Ideals must be backed by cannon, or left alone. With all submission to your Majesty, man is but a brute—we all devour each other if we can. Our rivals are sunk in the sloth of what is called humanitarianism. The new religion of so-called thinkers and feelers threatens to become a force which may so miseducate the masses that the workmen of the world may sweep away our own Culture of intellectual materialism by a universal strike for peace. This new movement, whose praise is being sung by poets and seers, must be throttled before its growth shall have become a menace to our Fatherland. Already the people are singing the hymns of the new religion of humanity in secret places. Socialism is rife in our land. Now is the moment to crush it for a hundred years and so preserve the ancient dynasty of which your Majesty is God's chosen head, and secure the supremacy of our race.

> [*Great cheers ring out from the square from many thousand voices. Here and there angry imprecations, too, are heard. The cheers come nearer and nearer, and the jingle-jingle of approaching cavalry is heard below.*]

RULER: Are they cheering me?

CHORUS OF MINISTERS AND PRINCES [*surrounding the* RULER]: They are cheering the war. They are cheering the Prince—he waves his hand to them.

RULER: Ingrates! Is my popularity, then, waning?

PRIME MINISTER [*his watch in hand*]: You are twelve minutes and fifteen seconds less popular than you were at midnight, your Majesty.

RULER [*twisting the quill pen in his hand*]: That is the voice of the people!

PRIEST: Vox populi, vox Dei!

WAR MINISTER: It is the voice of the Army!

> [*The Royal Dukes and Ministers, Priest, and Professor surround the* RULER, *cajoling, flattering, and browbeating him in turn. A military band blares out the National Hymn in which a hundred thousand voices join.*

The Ultimatum

The RULER *takes the pen once more; nerving himself to the great effort, he beckons to the* CHIROPODIST, *who makes to serve the liqueur.*]

CHIROPODIST: Now is my moment! [*Taking from his pocket the little bottle labelled " Poison," he is about to pour it into the glass, when a Royal Duke approaches him with something glittering in his hand.*]

ROYAL DUKE [*to* CHIROPODIST]: In recognition of your valuable services, his Majesty desires me to confer upon you the Order of the Golden Lamb, of the second class. [*Pins decoration on his breast.*]

CHIROPODIST [*overcome, mechanically, as in a dream, he clasps the bauble in his hand, then hesitates, gasping*]: O mother, mother!

RULER: It is war!

CHIROPODIST: Let it rip! [*He spills the poison on the floor.*]

[*The* RULER OF A GREAT PEOPLE *signs the Ultimatum. The* CHIROPODIST *shrugs his hump.*]

[*The Curtain falls.*]

September, 1914.

VII
The Fatal Fairy

VII

The Fatal Fairy

A LETTER WRITTEN TO A CHILD, DATED
MARIENBAD, JULY 30th, 1907

I KNOW you are interested in fairies, so I must tell you what happened this week. Of course, there are many people who do not believe in fairies, and I could not tell them of my experience, nor will you speak to such persons about what I am going to relate to you.

Fairies do not appear in the glare of the day, so I got up early in the morning, or, to be more particular as to facts, I sat up till dawn—because it is at dawn that fairies are least shy. It was at two o'clock on Tuesday morning that I stole out of the house and made my way to a glen of which I had been told by a shepherd who is on friendly terms with the fairies, because he plays to them on a pipe while they dance round him. This shepherd told me that fairies—which are supposed only to take joy in frolics—are really most useful. It is they who wake the cows in the morning by tickling their horns with hare-

Nothing Matters

bells; it is they who warn the deer that hunters are nearing, when they come down in the early morning to drink at the pool.

Well, at about a quarter to three I arrived at the glen, having provided myself plentifully with thistle-down, which the fairies love, for it is on thistle-down they ride the air; indeed, it is believed by some that from it they weave their wings. I sat down on a mossy mound and waited. The dawn had just begun, and my heart was beating quite loud with expectancy. I did not know what to do, but then I began to sing very softly (assuming, as best I could, the voice of a fairy), " Where the bee sucks, there lurk I." I thought this might attract them. Suddenly I heard the mooing of a cow in the valley, and I knew the fairies were at their work. I threw a handful of thistle-down in the air, when all at once six fairies were hovering above me, while another was swinging on a gossamer thread which floated between two pine trees. I pretended not to notice them, but went on humming the tune very softly, and they actually joined in the chorus.

I have never heard anything like it, except once when I heard shimmering whitebait (sea-fairies) singing under the water *à bouche fermée*. Soon I saw little faces peeping through the bracken and putting out their hands for thistle-

The Fatal Fairy

down, which I threw to them in plenty. What was really in my mind was to capture one of the fairies and to take it home. Never have I known a fairy to be caught by man by force. I thought that I would win by gentleness, so I sat smiling and bowing to and fro to them, very much as the Queen bows in her carriage. This seemed to please them, and they kept on bowing in return; but whether they did so in politeness or in mockery I could not tell. They would come up close to me, and then hop away like circumspect sparrows. Perhaps it was not right of me to covet the fairies, but there was one especially that took my fancy, for it had more confiding eyes than the others (their eyes are more sly than shy, and are always *twittering*). So I addressed myself in a very soft voice and in flattering terms to the fairy of my choice, but not too directly, lest the other fairies should be jealous, and to a strange humming sound which was going on all round me (a sound which was produced by their musical wings), I began telling them stories about the lives of men, and how great was their happiness.

I often spoke in the language of poets, pretending it was my own, and all the fairies sat round me in an admiring circle, and whenever I said anything unusually beautiful they turned somersaults in unison, which is their way of

Nothing Matters

expressing pleasure. I saw my little fairy had begun to trust me, for it turned a somersault up my leg and perched on my knee. I put my arm round its waist, and seized it to myself. At this moment a sunbeam shot through the trees, and to a strange and confused noise, all the other fairies disappeared. It is a remarkable assumption, but I believe it to be true, that when a fairy sympathises with a human being—a proceeding which in fairyland is regarded as most reprehensible—it becomes itself materialised, and in this state it remains until it is set free. But in this materialised form it will sometimes take strange shapes, as I soon learned, to my astonishment and cost.

Well, no sooner had all the fairies disappeared into the deeps of the wood than I began to make my way home, carefully secreting the captured fairy inside my waistcoat. Somehow, my conscience told me that it was not right to take a fairy from its home in the glen; but curiosity stifled my misgivings, and, persuading myself that it was my duty to my children to learn the ways of fairies, I quickly retraced my steps to my earthly home at the Green Cross, taking care that no one should see what I was carrying about with me. I admit that this was really an act of poaching, which even in poets is considered reprehensible. I have on occasion poached a

The Fatal Fairy

rabbit, I have even poached an egg, but never hitherto had I poached a fairy.

As I was nearing home I suddenly became aware of a fluttering inside my waistcoat, as though I had palpitation of the heart, and I immediately experienced a sensation of something sharp piercing my skin, and heard a most unfairylike squeak issuing from the same region. I put my hand inside my waistcoat, when, to my horror, I discovered that the fairy was no longer a fairy, but—what do you think?—it was a vulture: a bald-headed vulture! My heart stood still, and so did I! My clammy hand touched the cold, bald pate of the ill-omened bird. Its terrible beak squawked at me. I thought it was a nightmare. No; the blood on my finger was real human blood; the peck was undoubtedly that of a real bird. Too frightened to let my prisoner loose, I walked relentlessly on. Soon I was home, and, taking the flight of steps in one bound, as it seemed to me, I reached my room. Then followed a scene the like of which I have never known, waking or dreaming. As I write, though the thermometer registers 96 degrees, the perspiration freezes on my forehead, now and then dropping on the paper in the form of icicles! How appalling is sometimes the truth! But on with my tale.

My first act on entering my room was to close

Nothing Matters

the windows; then I turned the key in the door and let the bird loose. It was four o'clock, and I had had no sleep. I began to undress.

As I threw each garment down, the vulture seized it and tore it to pieces, and with the debris proceeded to make a nest in a corner of the room. I closed the shutters and went to bed, thinking that the darkness might produce sleep in my now loathed companion; but the darkness was even more terrible than the light, and there ensued an indescribable inferno * of sight and sound. I say sight advisedly, for in the dark the bird became lustrous. It began dancing a fandango round the room. I threw a boot at the awful form; the boot came straight back at my head. I flung a second; it hurtled against the window pane, which brittled to the ground. Suddenly the bird was sitting on my chest. I disappeared under the bedclothes. It danced on my body, chanting in a Cockney voice, with a Belgian accent, snatches of the Athanasian Creed! It was no nightmare; it is still to me a terrible reality. I gaze with envy on the toiling workman who does not believe in fairies. I look with an envious eye at the stolid, unintelligent policeman who passes me in the street. He knows no fairies. Oh, happy fool! Even the unsentient cabbage and the unperturbed turnip are objects

* Inferno—hell.

The Fatal Fairy

of envy. All the beauty of the world was turned to ugliness, for I had robbed fairyland. Bohemia, the cradle and the coffin of my crime, is a hated land to me. But I must not flinch from telling you of my sufferings, and of the bitter lesson they taught me. The bird had lifted its weight from my body, and I peeped through the bedclothes. The horrible inmate was dancing round the room, using the oaths of all the languages of the earth. I have travelled in many lands, but I have never heard so much bad language.

At the height of my feverish terror a remarkable discovery suddenly came to me. It is in moments of great mental excitement that our imagination throws bridges from one fact to another, and enables us to give to mankind the great scientific truths which solve the world's mysteries.

This is my discovery. Fairies are composed of feathers—and radium, that newly discovered power so rich in promise of future beneficence, so terrible in its vast potency to inflict blight and death over the face of the earth. There can be no doubt that this vital metal resides in fairies—that they are, indeed, the creation of this wondrous and mystic matter, which is capable of materialising the immaterial. It explains the whole existence of fairies, on whom scientific men have hitherto looked with doubt amounting to scepticism. But I will not seek to cloud your young mind

Nothing Matters

with the details of a theory, which I intend to embody shortly in an address to the British Institution, and which brings the radiumistic revelations into line with the other great postulates of scientific philosophy, and, furthermore, alone explains the strange havoc wrought by the fairy in the course of that, to me, eventful morning.

The weird inhabitant of my room gave out an extraordinary heat and a fierceness of light by the side of which that of the sun is but a shadowy shimmer. It lit up the room wherever it listed, sometimes burning on the walls, on the ceiling, and even illuminating wooden cupboards, which became transparent at its approach. I could not longer bear the surrounding darkness. I opened the window, and noticed that heads were peering out of all the windows in wonderment at the nocturnal pandemonium, for this awful bird never ceased shrieking. I bowed to the occupants of the hotel, and said " Good morning," as though nothing had happened. I looked round, and noticed that the vulture had emptied my inkpot at one gulp. Thinking to propitiate it, I threw it a beefsteak which lay upon my table, and it disappeared into the entrails of the beast with a gurgling sound. So far from being grateful, the creature only plucked tufts of my hair out by the roots.

The Fatal Fairy

This was too much, and I rang the bell. The night porter came, and called the night watchman, who called the policeman, who called the fire brigade; helter-skelter they all entered my room. And here is the extraordinary part of it all—they could see nothing! The beast huddled quiescent in a corner, with its red eyes staring at me through its legs! But they saw nothing. They sent for a doctor; he could see nothing, and put me to bed. I showed him the disordered room, the nest to which by this time my intruder had added the contents of the flock bed. All to no avail. He callously volunteered the suggestion that it was I who had caused the wreck in a delirium to which those who partake of the waters of Marienbad are sometimes prone. I pointed to my right hand, with which I had seized my victim; it was blistered all over with patches of purple and green. The man of medicine tried to look wise—in vain. They administered sleeping-draughts, but to no purpose. The bird kept me awake. I refused all food, and declined to be pacified until they brought me a large cage. And here is another remarkable link in this chain of incidents. The bird entered the cage with a curious, sardonic, but courtly bow.

The day had passed. Dusk was fast setting in. I made a resolve. That night I would lose the

Nothing Matters

bird. As it came, so it should go, or my peace of mind be for ever a remembrance. Strange to say, the bird remained quiet from the moment my resolve had been made. Over us both there reigned a calm—the calm of the victor on the one hand, the calm of the victim on the other.

The doctor called in the evening, felt my pulse, and with an unintelligent smile asked me if I still saw the bird. I did not deign to reply, for to vouchsafe vision to the blind is to court the arrogance of unbelief. I bowed as he said good night. So did the bird.

* * * * * *

Midnight had passed. I knew by the cool that the dawn was near. A strange squawk broke the silence—like a cock-crow aggravated by asthma. A flutter of wings told me to prepare. I dressed and, seizing the cage, crept silently out of the house and made my way to the glen. My limbs felt strangely weak, but I urged on with as much swiftness as they would carry me and my burden to the glen where the fairies dwell.

The mooing of a cow in the valley strikes my ear. We reach the glen. I can see the fairies dancing in the mist. I try to sing as fairies sing, but my vocal chords are unresponsive; my excitement chokes me. Softly, noiselessly, I place the cage upon the mossy mound where I sat yesterday.

The Fatal Fairy

What an interregnum of terror! Slowly, cautiously, I open the door of the cage. I see the bird with an abnormal fierceness of vision, then once more a horrible squawk, and it turns a somersault out of the cage into freedom.

By the time it has reached the ground it is no longer a vulture, but a fairy! Once more I throw the thistle-down in the air, and on its delicate fabric a fairy rides away. A peal of laughter from countless fairies rends the gossamer, a shaft of sunlight dispels the mist, and I am free once more.

* * * * * *

I should not have written at this length of my experience did not my tale contain a moral upon which you, my child, should ponder. It is this: One should never take a fairy to one's bosom lest it should turn into a bald-headed vulture; let not the rude hand of humanity seek to meddle with the intangible, which is real just so long as it is not touched by the dissolving breath of mortality.

VIII
Chapter One—a Fragment

VIII

Chapter One—a Fragment

THE events here recorded are now made public for the first time. Though the writer has been acquainted with them for many years, he has for obvious reasons refrained from mentioning them even in private; but the recent death of Julian Rodani, whose brief memoir appeared in the *Times* of September last has removed the only surviving actor in the drama set forth in these pages.

Julian Rodani, the last of his name, was always something of a mystery. Born of an Italian father and an English mother, he became an orphan at the age of ten. His education was amply provided for under his mother's will; he passed through Eton and Oxford, from which he emerged a somewhat sad and reserved youth. I made his acquaintance as a fellow-member of an artistic club, an acquaintance which rapidly ripened into friendship, and I owe this record to the familiarity of the small hours. About his father he was somewhat uncommunicative; but I understood that he died at the Battle of Sol-

Nothing Matters

ferino, when Julian was only a year old. His somewhat listless habit of mind he inherited from his mother, who never entirely recovered the shock of her husband's death. Nor did she ever mention his name, and Julian did not know whether his mother's silence was due to grief or to some mysterious cause which she did not venture to vouchsafe to her son.

I will endeavour to recall the incidents as faithfully as my memory will serve, in Julian Rodani's own words.

* * * * * *

JULIAN RODANI SPEAKS:

I will tell you the story of the most memorable Christmas Eve that I ever passed. I think it is not too much to say that the nightmare of it has never left me, and often I wake up drenched in perspiration at its remembrance.

I was invited to spend Christmas week at the house of Comte de Villemessant, in Normandy. I arrived at the railway station in a violent snow-storm. I had expected that a carriage would meet me; but it proved that the road was well-nigh impassable owing to the violence of the storm. In those days there were no motor-cars. At the neighbouring stables the ostlers refused to take out the horses on such a night, and I made up my mind to pass my Christmas Eve at the little

Chapter One—a Fragment

inn opposite the railway station. I was gazing disconsolately before me when a distinguished, white-haired old gentleman stepped towards me, and raising his hat in the Continental fashion, addressed me in French: " You appear to be in distress. Can I be of service to you ? "

I explained the situation to him, whereupon he said: " If you are going in my direction, I shall be delighted to give you a lift. May I inquire your destination ? "

I explained that I had intended going to the Château Ville-Mer, a distance of twelve miles.

" Then," said the stranger, " I can serve you indeed, for you are my fellow-guest, and I shall be delighted if you will share my travelling coach that I have brought with me on the train. It is a luxury which I permit myself since I am in somewhat delicate health."

At this moment an equipage with two horses drew up in front of us.

Never did I accept hospitality with greater gratitude. We proceeded on our journey. The night was intensely cold. I was famished, for I had had nothing to eat since early morning, and six o'clock had already struck. My host produced a silver case containing sandwiches of *pâté de foie gras* and of caviare, and politely urged me to partake of an old brandy of the

Nothing Matters

year 1859. Under its influence we quickly became voluble. The strange fascination of this old man, who spoke with a slight Italian accent, tempted me to enlarge upon every conceivable topic. He appeared interested in the opinions of a mere youth, given upon current events, social and political. His face was that of a diplomatist, his manner that of one habituated to courts. Only the scars on his face suggested a more militant occupation. The loneliness of the journey seemed to produce a sense of quick friendship between us.

"We must really finish the cognac," said my host. "It is the last material reminder of a memorable year. Let us drink to oblivion." He looked out of the window at the blizzard and gave a little sigh, followed by a hectic laugh.

"Yes," said I, by way of making conversation, "1859 was a memorable year on many accounts."

"The most memorable year of my life," said the old man, with a far-away look.

"The Battle of Solferino was fought in that year," I put in.

"Yes; that battle was memorable to me," said he, his clenched teeth biting the hairs of his short moustache.

At that moment we were passing a brilliantly lighted château on a neighbouring height. "That

Chapter One—a Fragment

château belongs to the De Coucelles family," my guide explained. "The old marquis, whom I knew intimately, was killed in a duel. It was a duel with swords."

A silence fell.

"Have you ever fought a duel?" I asked.

"Yes," he said, with a shrug of his shoulders and with his light, mirthless laugh. "I killed my man." He hummed a dry little tune, stroking his chin, which was slightly disfigured as though by the graze of a bullet long ago.

"Would it be impertinent to ask you to tell me your adventure?" I asked.

"Not at all," replied the old man. "Strange to say, I have never told the story to anyone, but I grow old and talkative. In youth one looks forward—in age one looks back."

"Was your opponent a Frenchman?" I asked.

"No," he replied; "he was an Italian—the greatest blackguard I ever knew. He died at the Battle of Solferino. But you would not be interested."

"Indeed I am," I urged; "but I think there are few conditions under which a man is justified in fighting a duel. You see, my education has been entirely English, and we have not the rigid code of honour that obtains among the great military nations."

Nothing Matters

"I think in my case," replied the old man dryly, "my action would have been justified in any country. Besides, in matters of honour, every man should be his own king."

"You make me curious," I replied, "for it is difficult for me to conceive any conditions that justify a man in taking another's life—unless it were for a woman's honour."

"Precisely," the old man ruminated. "Mine was a case of that kind. Well, to pass the time, I will tell you the story of my only duel. It was for a woman. The lady bore my name. When I was a young man I served in the Italian army. In the war between Austria and Italy one night after dinner we officers, after drinking to our king, made a vow that each of us would risk his life for any fellow officer of the regiment who was in danger. It was a curious vow, but it was a vow—a point of honour. I little thought how soon I should be put to the test. At the Battle of Solferino—it was a terrible battle—a troop of our regiment had been cut off, and it was reported that they were slain to a man. I was the youngest officer but one of the regiment —there was one younger. He was my dearest friend. He was the lieutenant in command of the unfortunate troop. I weary you—no? Well, at first the advantage was with the Austrians. We Italians were beaten back to our quarters of the

Chapter One—a Fragment

morning. Exhausted by the fatigue of the battle, we sat down; not one of us spoke. We ate and drank mechanically. I was numb with grief at the loss of my friend. Suddenly a post-bag was flung by an orderly into the room where we were seated, and each of us made for his letters. One was addressed in a strange hand to my friend whom we believed to be dead on the battlefield.

"As it would be necessary to send the news of his loss to the head of his family that night, and as nobody in the regiment knew his address, the colonel told me to open the letter of my comrade. I did so. Enclosed was another letter. It was addressed in my wife's handwriting. With trembling hands I broke the seal, and I knew their guilt—the guilt of my wife whom I loved, of my friend whom I revered. I had hardly time to realise the terrible doom that had fallen upon me, when the clattering of a horse's hoofs sounded in the courtyard. The rider was one of the missing troop. Covered with blood and foam, he told how he had galloped back from the field, how the company, although cut off, was not entirely annihilated, and how the few survivors were fighting hard with the enemy who surrounded them. My bosom friend was amongst them. I had listened without moving. My wife's letter was crushed in my hand. I made towards

Nothing Matters

the door, saying, ' Colonel, I am going to save him.'

"'But you ride to certain death,' the commander replied. My comrades echoed his words. I alone was unmoved. 'I am going to save him. I have given my word of honour.' Calmly, almost listlessly, I mounted my charger, determined to find my way to the house at the foot of a tower on a hill called ' The Spy of Italy.' It was a bright night. I made straight for the tower outlined against the horizon. Often on my way I was challenged by the enemy's sentries—often I felt the bullets whizzing past me; but I, whose soul was dead, bore a charmed life. I was like a drunken man—hardly heeding the sabre cuts that impeded my way. These cuts you see on my right cheek confirm my tale."

" That other on your chin ? "

" Ah, no ; that was a bullet wound. I am coming to that," the old man said. His face was ashen white, but he appeared strangely calm. " At this moment," he continued, " I saw him fighting by the side of two others. They were the last three : one fell from his horse, shot dead. The riderless horse galloped away over the dead bodies that surrounded us. Now the sergeant was sabred. Only *he* remained, his back against a tree.

"Bleeding profusely from my wounds, I made

Chapter One—a Fragment

one supreme effort, and with the accuracy of aim which comes to a man in great excitement, with my pistol I shot the hand that was upraised to kill him. The sword fell to the ground. My other pistol that was in my saddle I threw to my now defenceless comrade, while with my sword I pierced the body of his opponent. At this moment I realised that there was an onrush of fifty of the enemy infantry. There was not a moment to lose. In another fifty seconds we two would meet death in a common embrace.

"'Jump up,' I cried, and he half leapt, was half dragged, on to the neck of my horse. Amid a shower of bullets I turned the horse's head and galloped. It was the very irony of revenge. I, the saviour, grasped my demon in my arms. I galloped on and on, till we reached the foot of the hill where stood a shrine with the Madonna and Christ. We halted. I slipped from my saddle; my burden, too, alighted. By this time the night had darkened.

"'Let us cross ourselves,' I said, 'for one of us is going to die.' Having crossed himself, he came towards me with extended hand. My left hand was still clasping the woman's letter, now blood-stained.

"'Look,' I said. He knew it was the end. I heard his heart beating. I walked ten paces back. 'It is you or I.' The Madonna was

Nothing Matters

smiling down upon us. He had my pistol in his hand. He fired—you see the wound in the chin. The bullet glanced, hitting the crown of thorns that streamed with blood. Another moment and my wife's lover rolled to the ground a corpse. I kicked it; then I mounted my horse. Never was I so calm. I turned my horse's head—a grey stallion, I remember—as I thought, towards our camp. The horse turned back. Again I directed his head. We ambled on, and again the horse sought the opposite direction. I pulled his mouth until it bled. It is fate, I thought—what have I left to live for? Through the night we stumbled, and by the dawn I saw that the horse had led me home. They have strange instincts, these animals!

"I was back in the officers' quarters.

"'He is dead,' I said. Mass was said for his soul that morning. The stained letter I sent back to my wife without a word. I never saw the lady since."

"How awful!" I said. "How appalling!" The sweat seemed frozen on my hand. "Who was the scoundrel? Who was the man?"

"You would never have heard of him—the greatest blackguard I ever knew—a man named Rodani."

I sat like a ghost, with the calm of frenzy. The clanging of a bell wakened me. We had

Chapter One—a Fragment

arrived at our destination. The doors opened—
our host came towards us with extended hands.

" Ah, my dear Prince, I am honoured to welcome you to my house, old friend. And you have brought our young friend Rodani with you. I am delighted—you are already acquainted. Of course, you were his father's dearest friend . . ."

IX
The Cuckoo Clock

IX

The Cuckoo Clock

A CHRISTMAS STORY

THERE are some who believe in the transmigration of souls. There are many who speak disparagingly of cuckoo birds; indeed, the cuckoo is popularly supposed to be devoid of the very elements of mundane morality, for it will lay its eggs in the nests of others, to whom it will leave the trouble of hatching them; then will the sweet-voiced biped (too much an artist to be domestic) descend upon the nest, and casting the other birdlings from their legitimate resting-place, will annex the devastated home, with no more compunction, forsooth, than will a victorious nation a lesser. If, then, we accept the theory of the transmigration of souls (and did not the soul of Pythagoras inhabit a wild-fowl?), it may be surmised that into the bodies of cuckoos the souls of men may enter. Once we grant this, may it not be permitted to go a step farther—and to suppose it possible (in view of the latter-day wholesale

Nothing Matters

destruction of wild-birds) that the soul of some forgiving spirit may have sought refuge in the body of a cuckoo made of mortal hands and imprisoned within the four walls of a mechanical clock?

In an age of negation there will be many who will regard the following story of a cuckoo which returned good for evil and saved the life of the present writer as a material manifestation, coincidental rather than supernatural. They may even attribute the mysterious occurrences here recorded to the disordered brain of the author. My endeavour will not be to elucidate any occult theory, but rather by adorning a tale to point a moral which may be accepted or rejected, according to the temper and the intelligence of the reader.

It was a blear-eyed Christmas morning in the year 1880. The chemical fog which perennially hangs over the city of Glasgow was denser than ever, so it seemed to me, as I woke with a start, and peered through the dingy curtains at the drab, horizonless sky. Christmas Day in Glasgow City—and I not a Scot! I lighted what remained of a guttered candle, and by way of distracting my mind, sought by the flickering light to compose on the kaleidoscopic wallpaper a panorama of the Battle of Waterloo. Thrice in my imagination did I fight the battle through; then the

The Cuckoo Clock

candle gurgled out, and I was again in darkness. Once more I peered through the curtains for a gleam of sunshine, only to see a forlorn lamplighter in the act of lighting the gas-lamp on the opposite side of the street. A sense of suffocation, moral and physical, came over me, and a wild desire possessed me to fly the town and breathe the air of the open. Making a hasty toilet, I breakfastless groped my way down the stone staircase. In most of the Glasgow lodging-houses patronised by stage folk there is no front door, and it sometimes happens that at this festive season of the year the stairs become the refuge of belated revellers. Over such a one I stumbled in my descent, and fell headlong down the steps, knocking out an eye-tooth in my passage. On expressing to the prostrate but unperturbed Celt a hope that I had not disturbed his sleep, he begged me " not to mention it," and confided to me that he was " seeing in the New Year." (Scotsmen are rarely unpunctual in wassail.)

Grasping me firmly in an alcoholic grip, my new acquaintance refused to release me until I had joined him in singing " Should auld acquaintance be forgot." This I did.

On reaching the air I felt that this incident was a bad omen, and ever since I have been firmly convinced that it is unlucky to lose an eye-tooth on Christmas Day. The shock of the fall caused

Nothing Matters

a faintness which aggravated the fever already mastering me, but whose symptoms I did not realise at the time. I hailed a passing cab, drove to the landing-stage, and soon found myself on board a steamer, furrowing the Clyde. Our progress was slow owing to the fog. I was almost a solitary passenger, the only other occupant of the deck being one who exercised a strange influence on my overwrought nerves. I became aware of his presence without seeing him. A nausea beset me which, indifferent sailor though I was, I could scarcely attribute to the undulations of the Clyde. I felt that some uncanny force was behind me. I turned, and saw a weird-looking creature, whose lower face was almost hidden by a red muffler which had seen brighter days. His upper face was surmounted by an overhanging head-gear of fur, held together with hairpins. I saw only an eye—one eye—a terrible eye—a pink eye. I sat transfixed. The eye rose and came towards me; it looked all round me, but not at me. I examined the face closely, as a rabbit scrutinises a snake about to spring on it. Never had I seen so strange a phenomenon—the man had only one eye, and that squinted! The other eye was missing; I wondered how he lost it.

I was the first to speak.

"Do you mind not doing that?" I said.

The Cuckoo Clock

"What?" inquired the cyclops.

"That," I said, pointing to the roving optic, which looked like a lighted bell-buoy in a fog having lost its moorings. He merely winked. "What has become of the other?" I ventured tactfully, by way of making conversation.

"Lost it in the Balaclava Charge," replied the albino.

I thought he lied, but I had not the courage to say so at the time. He sat down beside me; I felt the cold sweat trickling down my spine.

"Travelling for pleasure?" he inquired.

"N-not exactly," I replied. My teeth chattered—all but the one I had lost on the stairs.

"Travelling on business?"

"Yes, my own business," I answered.

There was a silence of some minutes, during which my fellow-passenger of the pink eye drew from his cap three cards.

"You seem dull, young gentleman. Object to cards?"

I told him that it was one of my guiding principles never to play cards on Christmas Day.

"This is not exactly *playing* cards," he explained; "it is a game of guessing. More of an intellectual exercise than anything. Euclid, you know."

"Ah!" I said, fearing to thwart him. "That is a different thing."

Nothing Matters

"You see, this is the queen of diamonds," he went on; "ten shillings to five you can't spot which is the card."

I saw plainly where it was.

"Is not this what is called betting?" I asked.

He explained to me that betting was a matter of hazard—that if I could tell the card to a certainty, the element of gambling, in a strict sense, would be eliminated. This seemed to me a kind of hypocrisy, so by way of punishing him for a vice which it seemed to me should be discouraged, I said, "Very well, I take you—*that* is the card." And I took up the queen of diamonds.

"I bungled it that time," muttered the scoundrel to himself as he paid over the ten shillings.

Again I managed to pick out the queen of diamonds. Again and again my astonished companion paid me the ten shillings which I had so lightly acquired. We were nearing the landing-station, and I told the monster in the fur cap that I had reached my destination.

"Three more guesses," he cried. "Where is the queen of diamonds?" I distinctly saw it fall in the middle. "Double or quits this time!"

I assented, and picked up the ten of hearts!

The luck had turned, and by the time we touched the shore I had lost close upon five pounds. In the ordinary way such a sum would

The Cuckoo Clock

have been a formidable loss to me, but as it happened I had had a small legacy left me the week before, and having no banking account I carried the banknotes in my pocket—a foolish proceeding, as it proved. Drawing the five-pound note from the bundle, I handed it to my companion. I noticed that the eye lighted with an avaricious gleam upon the packet, which I hastily returned to my pocket.

"Double or quits again—I'll give you one more chance!" cried the man, holding me by the sleeve, as the boat bumped against the landing-stage.

"No, thank you," I said, for I began to suspect that there was an element of science in the luck of cards, a rule which I have since learnt extends to the other affairs of life. The man of the eye held me with a firm grasp; but with a dexterous jerk I freed myself and leapt on to the landing with a sense of intense relief and gratitude that my soul was still my own.

The sun's rays were dispelling the fetid mists that oozed from the earth, and I hurried to the inn to take some nourishment. In my progress I felt a faintness, which necessitated my holding on to the trees as I passed along. I reached the inn; I sat down; I felt a hot breathing down the back of my neck; I knew instinctively that

Nothing Matters

it was my gruesome friend of the boat! I started up, giving an involuntary scream, as one in a nightmare.

"Oh, it's you, my friend," I said, with an attempt at joviality. "But why are you here? I thought you were going on."

"I came after you to warn you, young man."

"Warn me!" I asked. What about?"

"About the money. Never carry banknotes in your pocket—that's all."

I thanked him effusively, and added that I should be sorry if his kindness should cause him to miss the boat. At that moment we saw her moving away.

"She's gone, and my carpet bag with her,' he cried.

I wondered what was in the carpet bag; I hoped a change of linen.

"Good-bye," I said; "I'm off."

"Where are you off to?" asked the albino.

"To—to Loch Laughlangluich," I said, inventing a name on the spur of the moment.

"Strange," said the stranger, "that's my pitch."

I knew he lied, for no such lake exists. I knew now, too, that the man would dog my footsteps if he could. I resolved to shake him off. This, I foresaw, was not to be done by force, for the man had an iron grip: his handshake was

The Cuckoo Clock

like some mediæval device for extorting secrets from martyrs. The greatest scoundrels I have ever known have an iron grip by which they gain a reputation for jolly good-fellowship; the most black-hearted men of my acquaintance invariably slap one on the back. Persuaded that physical force could not rid me of this man, I resorted to subterfuge.

"Our journey would be easier," said I, "if I could manage to hire two ponies; they are wonderful climbers—one for you and one for me. I will inquire at the stables."

My meal was still untasted, but I was indifferent to food; my only thought was to rid myself of the monster who, to my feverish brain, was momentarily growing more and more like a vampire whose acquaintance I had once made in a nightmare. I waved a hand, as much as to say, "I shall be back soon," and made for the stables. Once in the open air, I took to my heels and ran through the woods uphill as hard as I could. I had run for fully twenty minutes when I halted for a moment. I looked back for the first time. I fancied I saw the figure of a man gliding along among the trees. My heart stopped beating. I looked again—the man was not to be seen. It must have been my imagination, I thought. I felt giddy, my head was thumping like a threshing machine, and I realised for the

Nothing Matters

first time that I was in a fever. At this moment I saw something moving through the thick underwood—it *was* the vampire stealing towards me. Should I stay and face him? I could already feel his iron grip round my throat. Should I surrender to him, offering to share with him the banknotes against which my heart was beating so that I could hear their rustle? No; I would go quietly on, as though I had noticed nothing, and by a brilliant stroke of strategy I would make a dash for freedom. I walked leisurely on, not looking back, but listening for a falling footstep behind me. All was still. I continued my journey. Suddenly the sound of rushing water broke upon my ear—it was a mountain stream which had swollen to a torrent. I made for it. The opposite side was precipitous. I would venture it and put the stream between me and my pursuer—if indeed I was pursued. I descended the slope—I leapt the stream, and was safely on the other side. I heard a hoarse laugh above—the man of the pink eye was descending the slope.

"I thought you'd want a guide," he shouted to me. "I'll be with you in a minute."

There seemed no escape. I could not scale the steep ascent. Something struck my face: it was the branch of a tree whose arm seemed providentially extended to me from above. I caught on

The Cuckoo Clock

to it, and pulled myself up as by a rope, hand over hand. I noticed that my pursuer had gained my side of the stream, but not without a ducking. I had reached the top of the precipitous ascent. I felt a pull at the end of the root, like the bite of a fish at a line. The man was evidently following my example. Would the tree carry his weight? It seemed to have almost cracked under mine. Our united weights would certainly cause it to break. My pursuer was already half-way up. Taking hold of the branch, I threw all my weight on to it. *Crash—bang—*the branch fell. I looked over—the man was in the water. I thanked God, for I was safe. I would make my way back by a circuitous route as quickly as I could, for the snow was beginning to fall, and dusk would soon set in. Was the man drowned? I hoped he was. Was I his murderer? How would the jury bring in their verdict? Justifiable homicide, I hoped. I remembered that I had lost my hat—that would identify me with the crime. While I was running, I heard the judge summing up against me—I heard him pronounce sentence of death upon me—in a strong nonconformist Scottish accent, too, which seemed to add another terror to death. I noticed that the judge had one eye that squinted through me—and it was the colour of pink. I stopped and listened, not for the judge's words—for

Nothing Matters

they had ceased—but the footsteps of Death behind me. All was still save for the falling snow.

Dusk had set in. My throat was dry. I ate some snow—it tasted like inferior sawdust. I noticed that I was wet to the skin; the perspiration froze upon me. I shivered and sat down. I had lost my way, I reflected. The dusk grew denser; my teeth were chattering; an ague had stolen over my limbs. I tried to move them, but it seemed as though the joints were frozen. Still I sat staring before me. What would happen to me? A dim pink light seemed to shine through the neighbouring bracken. Was it the eye of my pursuer? I stared and stared. The light became more vivid. It did not blink—it could therefore not be an eye. Was it the light of a house? I raised myself by the aid of a tree. I peered forth. The light was shed from a hut on the hill opposite. I would make an effort to gain it. Like a drunken man, I stumbled from tree to tree; now and then my knees gave way, and I fell; the cold was intense. Icicles were hanging from my hatless hair, but I was nearing my goal. Suddenly the light went out, and darkness came again. I groped on, trusting to instinct to guide me. My head struck something—it was a door. I fell heavily against it. I heard the click of

The Cuckoo Clock

pattens descending a stair—I saw a light shining through the chinks of the wood; a bolt was withdrawn, and a woman stood shading her eyes. A brick floor seemed to rise and strike my forehead. "Lord 'a' mercy," said the woman's voice, "wha's thus?" (which is Scotch for "Who's this?"). "It's me," I said (in such moments even grammar deserts one). "Drunk again!" she replied, probably thinking it was her peccant husband. I assured her I was only dying, and all I wanted was a bed. "Bed, mon, I haven't a bed—the last bed was let to a party but half an hour ago." I heard a snore that seemed to shake the rafters like some volcanic upheaval. The woman suggested I should resume my journey. This I assured her was impossible. She put her candle to my face.

"Lor-r-rd 'a' mercy," she cried, "you look like a ghost. Come in."

could not move. She dragged me over the threshold and put me before the fire, which was burning low.

"You're in a fever," she said. "My boy went off in just such a one."

She helped to undress me, fetched some straw, which she explained was the only bed she could afford that night; poured some whisky down my throat; in her tactful way expressed the hope that I might "leeve through the naicht,"

Nothing Matters

and left me to myself. On ascending the stairs, the good woman stumbled; the snoring above suddenly ceased: the sleeper had evidently awakened. By the flickering firelight I fancied I saw the figure of a man peering down. I gave a scream.

"Don't be afeered," said the woman. "It's only the other gentleman."

I wondered what the other gentleman was like. I composed myself to rest for the night, placing my watch and chain and the banknotes under the straw at my head. The terrors of that night will never be effaced from my memory. The fever was burning me inside; outside was icy cold. All the experiences of my life from my earliest childhood were rushing pell-mell through my brain. Continually I started up and fought with imaginary wild beasts, only to sink down again exhausted on the straw. The windows rattled, the crickets seemed to shriek; at intervals the stentorian snore above vibrated through me like a tenement shaken by an underground railway. But of all the terrible sounds I heard that night, the most terrible was the sound of a cuckoo-clock which hung above me on the wall.

"Cuckoo, cuckoo, cuckoo, cuckoo, cuckoo, cuckoo, cuckoo, cuckoo!" shrieked the bird; it was eight o'clock. I knew that the bird would

The Cuckoo Clock

haunt the night; it was the most awesome sound I had ever heard. In fever, sound and sight become magnified a thousandfold. I lay trembling in wait for the next hour to strike. Nine o'clock struck—an eternity happened, and it was ten. I was a hiding criminal—the cuckoo was my conscience. A blackbeetle climbed up and sat upon my chest—by the light of the fire I watched it; it deliberately got on its hind legs and made faces at me. I saw each expression distinctly—and, terrible to relate, the beetle had only one eye—that eye was pink—and squinted! (I have since been assured by an eminent entomologist that an albino blackbeetle is absolutely a unique specimen.) I did not dare to move, but lay waiting patiently for the next strike of the clock. I watched for those terrible doors to open and let forth the bird which should bow to me ironically eleven times, and then once more disappear into its prison.

The face of the clock was growing larger and larger. A terrible impulse beset me. I could no longer bear the torture of the cuckoo. I resolved to kill the bird. My eye fell on a steel knitting-needle wherewith my hostess had been knitting. I seized it—I determined to spring upon my tormentor and to put an end to my sufferings. What was one murder more?

The hand of the clock was moving slowly

Nothing Matters

towards eleven. The gates opened with a terrible clang, the bird darted forth from its lair and shrieked at me.

With one great effort I gathered together what strength was left me, and at the tenth stroke plunged the cold steel into the cuckoo's throat. With something between a yell and the gurgle of a dislocated thorax, my tormentor disappeared into darkness, and all was still. I fell back upon the straw, exhausted, spent. A numbness took possession of my limbs; but, strange to say, my mind became clear, even as a calm will come over the mind of the criminal as he essays his last walk to the gallows. The crisis of my fever had evidently gone by.

The next hour passed uneventfully. The snoring above had ceased, I noticed, and now and then I could hear the tread of one walking about the room overhead. I began to review the happenings of the day sanely. My nerves were no longer disturbed by the chirping of the cricket or the ticking of the clock. It could not be far from midnight. Sleep began to steal over me, when I heard the creaking of the stairs which led from the chamber above. A stealthy, noiseless step, as of someone creeping down in his socks, accompanied the creaking. I was conscious that the intruder was standing still as though listening. I held my breath.

The Cuckoo Clock

The figure began to move about the room, evidently in search of some object.

The embers of the fire were burning low, but I could just make out that the form was that of a man and not of a woman. It was stooping low to pick up something—that something was my coat. The garment was dropped and another taken up. I realised that my pockets were being rifled. I remembered that my watch and banknotes were under my head.

A pink eye advanced slowly towards me.

I dared not scream, for I should have been powerless to protect myself, so I breathed quietly as though in sleep. I then was conscious of a hand stealing through the straw and approaching nearer and nearer to my head. I gave an involuntary gasp, and opened my eyes. As I did so, a stray moonbeam shining through the chink of the door showed a knife raised above me.

And then the most terrible and unearthly noise I have ever heard burst from above—a shriek as of a thousand demons let loose from Hell—a yell which would have affrighted the consciences of all the Herods.

It was the cry of the wounded soul within the cuckoo-clock.

A scream rose to the lips of the murderer, the uplifted knife fell harmless by my side, and in another moment I saw the affrighted form

Nothing Matters

of the one-eyed albino rushing through the door into the night. Still the voice shrieked after the departing form. Twelve times it shrieked. There was a terrible click as of the closing of gates. And then oblivion.

Rest came to me that night. The cuckoo's voice was silenced, perhaps for ever. But every Christmas Eve, when the clock strikes twelve, I give a thought to the soul which had entered the body of the wounded toy cuckoo that saved my life.

X
God is Good

X
God is Good

IT was a dreary, steamy Christmas morning in a northern suburb of London. From the roof of No. 11 Jabez Terrace the rain dripped in gelatinous drops, hastening the decay of the crumbling stucco. From the little corrugated iron chapel opposite a cracked and consumptive bell was tinkling a doleful message of peace and good will towards miserable sinners—the roadway to salvation was cumbered by a dead cat and a derelict tin can.

Inside the parlour bedroom of No. 11 Jabez Terrace sat a young woman vainly endeavouring to feed the newly-born baby at her breast—feebly the child whimpered his hunger. The mother had not the wherewithal to buy the milk from the dairy hard-by. Nothing pawnable was left in the bare room. The " Emporium " in which she had been employed had refused to allow her to return to her work; her errand in quest of other employment had been in vain, and on Christmas Eve she had returned home empty-handed—save for a hectic geranium which she had

Nothing Matters

found on the floor of an omnibus. The flower, reposing in a broken mug, used as a substitute for a tooth-glass, was the only decoration the room could boast.

The child's father was among the " missing." The last letter the young woman had received months ago told her how he intended to " act honourable " by her on his return. This letter, now in fragments, she was once more spelling out by the light of a spluttering little paraffin lamp whose smell vied for supremacy with the fumes belched by the enfeebled wind from the neighbouring brickfield.

The girl sought to pacify her baby by singing a half-remembered little Christmas hymn, but her throat was tired, and she ceased. The room was still—the canary lay dead in its cage. The breakfastless mother fell back on the unmade bed and moaned: she was too numb to fight; she had not the heart to beg; she had not the strength to steal. She only gazed dry-eyed through the weeping window-pane. " God help us," was her prayer. There was the shuffle of a heavy foot-tread on the pavement. " Old clo'! Old clo'! " the only human Christmas greeting she had heard, broke the silence.

The face of an old man, as of the wandering Jew masquerading as Father Christmas, leered through the window-pane. " Old clo'! " the

God is Good

voice croaked again. The girl shook her head. Then the apparition tapped at the window-pane, and with crooked finger pointed towards some object in the room. The young woman threw up the sash.

"Vat'll you take for de broken mug, young lady?"

The ravenous Father Christmas, having examined the mug, knew it to be a rare find—which he could turn into bank-notes. To the girl it was a worthless gift left by a grandmother.

"What will you give me for it?" she asked.

"Well, my dear, it's Christmas time, and that makes me soft-hearted—here's two silver half-crowns for you—you can keep the geranium for luck."

"Oh, thank you, sir," said the girl.

The gaunt figure passed on. "Old clo'! Old clo'!" was heard fainter and fainter, as nearer and nearer came the cry, "Milk below!"

The starving mother seized her child in her arms and sank upon her knees.

"God is good," she sobbed.

And "Milk below!" sounded as a message from Heaven above.

After=thought

IN looking through these proofs I have been haunted by the vague apprehension of uncommitted crime. Have any of the plots of my stories been prophetically plagiarised by those who have gone before ? A friend of mine lately asked me, in terms of no measured reproach, why I never read books, to which I answered, " I am afraid of cramping my style."

On this ground, I plead the innocence of ignorance.

H. B. T.

XI
The Importance of Humour in Tragedy

XI

The Importance of Humour in Tragedy

(PRESIDENTIAL ADDRESS DELIVERED AT THE BIRMINGHAM MIDLAND INSTITUTE, 1915)

WHEN you honoured me by making me your President for the year 1915, and when I chose for my address, " The Importance of Humour in Tragedy," I little thought of the ironic application of that title to the conditions which surround us to-day. " This was sometime a paradox, but now the time gives it proof," for assuredly its importance was never so great as now, the most momentous moment of the world's history.

At the very hour when the new religion of humanity seemed to be knocking at the gates of the world's conscience; when the dreams of idealists, the humanising influences of the arts were asserting their sway, and the vanities of potentates and tyrants were being swept away to the dust-heap of antiquity; when the light of a new civilisation seemed to be quivering on the horizon—at that very hour was the world plunged into darkness, at that very hour was it

Nothing Matters

hurled back past the Middle Ages, and on the vacant throne of Right sits Folly smiling at Chaos. At this time it is only the force and calm of humour which can stay us from crossing the borderland which separates despair from madness. But for humour we should go mad. Sanity is humour.

In this spirit, here are you, ladies and gentlemen, assembled to listen to an address by a player philosophising on the importance of humour in tragedy.

If the quality of humour is important in comedy, it is, I venture to say, yet more important in tragedy, whether it be in the tragedy of life or in the tragedy of the theatre.

Were I asked what companion I would choose to start on life's journey in quest of happiness, I would unhesitatingly summon to my side humour—Humour, the darling love-child of Intelligence. As instinct is greater than learning, as intelligence is greater than intellect, so is humour greater than wit. Wit has its birth in the head of intellect, humour in the heart of intelligence. Humour is the power of self-criticism—it enables us to estimate men and events at their true value. It is the touchstone which distinguishes the real from the sham in art. As in art so in life. Humour helps us to bear with injustice, to laugh at pretension, to behave with modesty in success, and to face adversity with

Humour in Tragedy

calm. The man who has it will not lose his dignity in emergency. In the great tragedy of life's end he will meet even Death with a smile.

It always seems to me that there is a fine spirit of humour in the famous epitaph in Hull churchyard on the grave of one Martin Elginbrod:

> "Here lie I, Martin Elginbrod:
> Have mercy on my soul, O God,
> As I would if I were God
> And thou wert Martin Elginbrod."

People are too apt to treat God as if He were a minor royalty.

I take it that the main object of man is to find happiness—each after his own fashion. By happiness I do not mean pleasure, for which it is sometimes mistaken—indeed, in pursuing the phantom of pleasure we often lose the substance of happiness. Happiness is a condition of the mind, and does not depend on conditions of pleasure. It is in ourselves: it is a kind of self-hypnotism. Humour helps us to attain this condition of mind which we call content. Some will find happiness in a debauch of pessimism—they "enjoy bad health," as the charwoman said. Persons of a certain order of mind will extract a perverse kind of joy from attending the funeral of a complete stranger. Such an

Nothing Matters

event becomes a holiday treat to the born pessimist. To what base uses do the poor resort in quest of happiness; but I suppose the only joy of life vouchsafed to many of these is the cessation of pain. Thank God, the toiling masses are given to-day greater opportunities of human joys than in the "good old days" when their nearest approach to sweetness and light was to be found in the public-house.

Humour being an attitude of mind, it can to a certain extent be developed. Given the seed, it can be cultivated. I remember a valued friend once said, "Life is a mirror: smile at it and it will smile back; frown at it and it will frown again."

Children should be taught lessons in happiness; that, for instance, it is not a sin to be joyous, any more than it is a virtue to be miserable. A kind of Pagan spirituality has of late years taken the place of the "Fee, fi, fo, fum" brimstone teaching of our Victorian childhood—though I confess that long before I had ceased to crack nuts with my teeth I had given up the doctrine of "Open your mouth and shut your eyes."

It may at once be granted that, like every other precious force (like radium and electricity), the force of humour can be misapplied, and so become dangerous; it is undeniable, too, that

Humour in Tragedy

an absence of humour will enable men to reach the goal of their ambition more quickly, for they who see only what is immediately in front of their noses will often outstrip in the race those who are hampered with humour and the sensitiveness and love of life which that humour implies. The earnest worldling keeps his eye on his main chance, blinkered to the life that passes him, and sallies forth on his way undismayed by snubs, impervious to criticism, undaunted by ridicule, deaf to the song of the siren, unmindful of the by-lanes where primroses beckon the passer-by to linger in pleasant dalliance.

> "A primrose by a river's brim
> A yellow primrose was to him,
> And it was nothing more."

"And what in the name of common sense should it be more?" exclaims the man in the street, who is generally the man *of* the street. There let us leave him.

Certainly, humour may be a clog in the game of life. On the other hand, he who is gifted with it will laugh at the bludgeonings of fate. The man who yields to the assaults of adversity is often stronger than he who offers them a rigid resistance. Iron breaks, steel bends and recovers its equipoise.

Humour assuages pain, though I am bound

Nothing Matters

to say I have found it inefficacious in toothache or in sea-sickness. Thus we see that philosophy has its limitations. Our humour is apt to stop short at ourselves—that is the tragedy of life. The misfortunes of others we bear more philosophically. The supreme test of humour is in its personal application. It is the quintessence of humour which enables a man to laugh at himself and gives him his highest dignity, for he who can laugh at himself must needs be gifted with a tolerance, a pity for others. None so sensitive to criticism as those whose business it is to ridicule others. True humour is rarely cruel; cruelty and sarcasm belong rather to the domain of wit. Nothing will appeal to an audience's sense of the ridiculous so much as the fall of the decrepit pantaloon on the butter-slide prepared by the wily clown. But that is not humour.

A homely illustration of the difference between wit and humour came within my knowledge. I have two friends—one a wit, the other a humorist. They were staying at a country inn and retired to their rooms in high spirits. A. conceived the brilliant idea of changing all the boots that were put outside along the passage. He did so. (That was wit.) B. thought of the inconvenience that this derangement would entail on the victims of his friend's ingenuity, and,

Humour in Tragedy

without telling A., lest he should deprive him of his triumph, changed all the boots back to their rightful owners' doors. (That was humour.) You will say these are not brilliant examples of wit or humour—you are right. 'Tis but a homespun fable.

Humour, like love, cannot be bought; it is common to the peasant and the king, to the prelate and the 'bus-conductor. Between those who have it there exists a kind of freemasonry; it is the touch of nature which makes the whole world kin. I believe that humour is unofficially and secretly possessed by both political parties. I remember sitting at a table at which were gathered distinguished men, Conservatives and Liberals. Turning to my neighbour I said:

"Is it not curious that all these sitting here appear to think alike to-night on every conceivable subject, while in their public utterances they differ so violently?"

"Yes," replied my friend; "but this is our holiday. Here we are allowed to speak the truth, for humour is in the chair—*and there are no reporters.*"

In public life nothing is so suspect as humour. Perhaps that is why so many men scruple to tell the truth in public.

One blessing the war has brought to us—the abolition of parties. I have never been able to

Nothing Matters

understand why parties should exist. If every man acted according to his conscience, clarified by humour, there would be no necessity for the barbed red-tape entanglements which divided Englishmen in deadly enmity. If a plain man ventured before the war to express a merely human opinion on some great social question which came within the range of politics, he was liable to be dubbed a "ruddy Radical" on the one side or a "gory Tory" on the other. A common cause and a common humour unites all classes in a great brotherhood to-day.

Is humour possessed by the greatest statesmen, the greatest thinkers, the greatest conquerors of the world ? In the course of my remarks I shall be so bold as to attempt to grapple with this fascinating problem. But, first, it is necessary to arrive at a definition of humour, for I believe there are many. Humour at its highest is, I take it, a nice balance of the mind, an intellectual poise. It is an attitude towards life and all that pertains to it—the faculty of regarding the events of life philosophically, the habit of looking at things with a certain tolerance, a restrained gaiety. Wisdom is thought plus humour.

A sense of humour would paralyse the arm of the murderer, and prevent its possessor from embarking upon a deliberate career of wholesale

Humour in Tragedy

wreckage and destruction. His sanity would revolt against the idea of conduct in man which would be reprobated in most of his fellow animals in the Zoological Gardens. The person gifted with humour will feel that if it is wrong to kill one man it is ten thousand times more wrong to kill ten thousand men. But this logic has not yet reached the legislators of the world; in International affairs Christianity and humour go to the wall at the bidding of expediency. If the divine right of humour were bestowed on monarchs there would be no war. To stop the madness of war even the ties of royal blood-relationship are unavailing. Blood is thicker than water, but gold is thicker than blood. Beware when monarchs kiss!—soon comes the tug of war.

In saying that our sense of humour stops short at ourselves in the ordinary affairs of life, I recall an instance which was related to me by one who has the medical care of the inmates of Broadmoor. This story shows that the point of view of normally sane persons is apt to lapse from sanity at the lure of vanity. My medical friend escorted on two successive occasions two distinguished visitors who were interested in the condition of his patients. The first visitor (Mr. Smith) was a young man who expressed a desire to be presented among others to one whose ambi-

Nothing Matters

tion in life had proved to be a too wholesale extermination of the human race.

"Be polite to him," said my friend, "for he is the most dangerous inmate of this asylum. Mr. Gallstone," he proceeded, "let me present to you my friend, Mr. Smith."

"Take off your hat, sir," said the criminal. Mr. Smith took off his hat. "Turn your profile, sir," continued Mr. Gallstone. Mr. Smith turned his profile. Mr. Gallstone exclaimed, "A truly noble Aryan type, the forehead of a poet laureate, nobility of feature, a generous mouth, a personality which should be the cynosure of womanhood, a born leader of men. You have an eye, sir, which shows the fire of the idealist held in check only by the power of logic. You will go far, sir; you will go far. Put on your hat, damn you, and pace forth to victory!"

Mr. Smith replaced his hat. In leaving the premises he turned to my doctor friend and said:

"I have been greatly interested by all I have seen; but there is one case in which I think the patient may be unjustly detained. Is it not possible that a grave error of judgment may have been committed?"

"To which case do you refer?" inquired the doctor.

"I refer to the case of a Mr. Gallstone, who

Humour in Tragedy

appeared to me remarkably intelligent," said the young man sympathetically as he took his leave.

The next week a distinguished permanent official of the public service paid a visit to the prison. He, too, was escorted by my friend.

"Mr. Gallstone," said he, "allow me to present to you my friend, Sir William Jones."

"Take off your hat, sir," said Mr. Gallstone, "and make yourself at home here."

Sir William removed his hat and tried to look at home.

"Any relation of the celebrated thinker and philosopher of that name?" inquired Mr. Gallstone.

"Yes," replied Sir William; "I am his son."

"Remarkably paltry head for the son of so great a man. Put on your hat, sir," said Mr. Gallstone, as he turned to finish a game of solo dominoes.

Sir William, in bidding farewell, took the doctor aside and said:

"I have been deeply interested in all I have seen, but I have never been so shocked with the depraved criminality of a fellow-being as I was to-day."

"To what case do you refer?" asked the doctor.

"I refer to the case of Gallstone. I wonder you don't put him in irons!"

Nothing Matters

Points of view differ. Our humour stops short at ourselves.

It is a fact, by the by, which I have observed in life, that all madmen are singularly deficient in the quality of humour. I have noticed that an inordinate conceit characterises that sad state. I presume it is because the sense of proportion is distorted. Persons without a sense of humour always write long letters; and I have noticed, too, that all madmen write letters of more than four pages. I will not venture to assert that all persons who write more than four-paged letters are mad. Still, the symptom should be watched.

One of the most alarming signs of insanity, it has often seemed to me, is that of writing to the newspapers (invariably more than four written pages) to prove that Hamlet was mad, and that Bacon wrote Shakespeare. Yet the same writers who scorn the idea that Hamlet pretended to be mad generally assert with equal vehemence that Shakespeare pretended to write the works of Bacon. I am satisfied that many of the learned commentators have only been kept out of lunatic asylums by the energy which they have expended in the harmless occupation of discussing these two kindred subjects in print. In many cases it has proved a most valuable safety-valve.

Though the subject of the Shakespeare-Bacon

Humour in Tragedy

controversy is somewhat musty, I will ask you to bear with me while I wander down a by-lane of parenthesis in order to prove to my own entire satisfaction that, tested by the touchstone of humour, the Bacon theory vanishes into the air. If there is one quality which characterises the writings of Shakespeare more than another it is humour. He cannot resist it—it is irresistible. Humour, like murder, will out. Had Bacon humour? I think not.

Bacon had learning, Shakespeare not much. But he had instinct. Some people are born educated; Shakespeare inherited the knowledge of his forefathers, and he possessed an unexplored power of assimilating all that came in his way. He made precisely the mistakes that Bacon would never have made. Book-learning is not wisdom. Shakespeare himself ridicules this most whimsically in *Love's Labour's Lost:*

"Study is like the Heaven's glorious sun,
    That will not be deep-searched with saucy looks;
Small have continual plodders ever won,
    Save base authority from others' books."

The King replies:

"How well he's read, to reason against reading!"

How small a thing is education save for those who have the imagination to illuminate it! Too much reading is certainly a hindrance to the

Nothing Matters

development of the imagination. Instead of giving birth to original thoughts, the man who has only reading gets to think by quotation—he relies on the cold storage of memory.

Many years ago I met at the house of a friend an eminent cryptogrammatist who had written a work proving by algebra that Bacon wrote Shakespeare. I made so bold as to ask him whether Bacon wrote the Shakespeare Sonnets. He replied that his case rested on that certainty. I pointed out to him that while it was conceivable that Francis Bacon, for political reasons, did not wish to acknowledge the authorship of the plays, it was inconceivable that in the outpourings of his soul in the Sonnets he should call himself " Your own sweet will," constantly punning on the Christian name of his paid " ghost "—the vulgar poacher-butcher-actor-manager.

Again, look here upon this picture and on this: Could he who had proved himself a heartless advocate, who sacrificed the Earl of Essex, and after the grave had closed over him published a vile attack upon his dead friend and benefactor, " like wrath in death and envy afterwards "— could he whose meanness was aggravated by respectability, who had paddled long in the putrescent puddles of politics, till right and wrong were merged in the melting-pot of expediency—could he have written these words ?

Humour in Tragedy

"Tired with all these, for restful death I cry,
   As, to behold desert a beggar born,
And needy nothing trimm'd in jollity,
   And purest faith unhappily forsworn,
And gilded honour shamefully misplaced,
   And maiden virtue rudely strumpeted,
And right perfection, wrongfully disgraced,
   And strength by limping sway disabled,
And art made tongue-tied by authority,
   And folly, doctor-like, controlling skill,
And simple truth miscall'd simplicity,
   And captive good attending captain ill:
      Tired with all these, from these would I be
         gone,
      Save that, to die I leave my love alone."

Is there in any of Bacon's works one hint of this sweet humour, this noble scorn, this glowing melancholy which breathes throughout the works of Shakespeare? I think not. Writers more dissimilar than these two cannot be found. There is one thing quite certain: that if Bacon wrote Shakespeare, then Shakespeare must have written Bacon!

But to return to my text. In its essentials, the oil of humour is the same throughout the world as is the essential vinegar of wit; but each nationality has its own characteristic humour, and though it is perhaps pre-eminently developed in the Anglo-Saxon race, I have found it in the Arab and the Japanese. The Japanese are a peculiarly

Nothing Matters

smiling people. There is a Japanese proverb which says, "A melancholy face is stung by the bees." Another Japanese proverb contains excellent advice to intending suicides: "When you take poison, don't lick the plate."

Humour is everywhere; it can be picked off the hedges of the highway. A gipsy was asked by a friend of mine:

"How do you decide which way to go next?"

"I turn my back to the wind," replied the gipsy.

An excellent piece of philosophy! Yes; humour is a gipsy—it has no country; though there *are* Englishmen who deny true merit to the humour of America, whose peculiarly attractive characteristic is that it leaves something to the imagination of the listener. A curious instance of this British intolerance was given me by a brilliant American friend. A stolid Englishman was his guest, and would listen to the American's prolific anecdotage with the mild and surprised courtesy of fatigue. On his way to the station at the conclusion of his visit, the Englishman, while thanking his host for his hospitality, confided to him that he deeply regretted that he had been unable to appreciate the characteristic humour with which the American had sought to outvie the Englishman's brilliant flashes of silence.

Humour in Tragedy

"Now tell me," said the taciturn Saxon, "one story which you really consider a true sample of American humour, and I give you my word of honour as an English gentleman that I will do my best to appreciate it."

My American friend drew up his dogcart and proceeded:

"Well, it was a rainy Sunday at St. Louis, and the public-houses were shut. A stranger stood on the corner of the street wanting to post a letter home.

"'Do you know where the post office is?' he inquired of a passer-by.

"'Yes,' replied the man, and walked on. But on reflection he took pity on his fellow-man, and retraced his steps to the place where the stranger was still standing in the rain, disconsolately whistling to the wind. 'Do you really want to know where the post office is?' he asked.

"'No,' said the stranger, and walked on."

"Well," said the Englishman, "I think they were both extremely rude." There ensued a silence so deep that you could almost hear it.

In life humour enables us to rate ourselves and our own acts at their true value; it helps us to discount flattery. Flattery makes the great little, the little never great. "Oh, that men should be to counsel deaf, but not to flattery." We are none of us entirely proof against flattery,

Nothing Matters

which is the cheapest form of bribery; it is largely employed by lower organisms as a means of self-propulsion. Flattery is a passport to the human heart; few of us can resist its gilded key. I have known people of quite mediocre intelligence who have managed to succeed in life by judicious flattery. To illustrate this form of worldly wisdom I may record an incident which almost happened. I met a former acquaintance in Piccadilly:

"How well you're looking," said he.

"Well, you're not looking very well," said I.

"That's hardly a tactful observation," he retorted. "I ought to be looking well, for I'm a millionaire."

I expressed my astonishment.

"How on earth did a man of your contemptible brains manage to achieve that happy state, while one of my relative brilliance is still struggling with adversity?"

"Are you doing anything to-night?" he asked.

"No," I replied.

"Then let us dine together and I will tell you all about it."

I consented.

I met my friend at the appointed hour, and he greeted me by telling me that I looked extraordinarily well. There was little conversation, for

Humour in Tragedy

silence, the wisdom of fools, was possessed by my friend in a supreme degree.

With the familiarity which is distilled from Château Yquem I pressed my supposed host at the end of the feast to enlighten me as to the elixir which enabled a man to enter through the needle's eye of poverty into the kingdom of the rich.

"Well," said the dullard, "I will tell you—my formula is a very simple one. I greeted all my acquaintances with the words, 'How well you're looking!' Thus I made many friends and propitiated even my enemies. Gradually invitations came to me, people put me into their 'good things' on the Stock Exchange; I became, in fact, a social *persona grata*. I held my tongue—men thought me wise, and I became a millionaire. That is my secret. Try it, my dear fellow. How well you're looking!" And he left me to pay the bill.

Truly, it is the poor man that payeth for the rich man's dinner!

Humour teaches us many things; it teaches us the equality of man; the true gentleman is he whose courtesy is not regulated by his interests. The *grand seigneur* has the same manner for the great and for the little. But here again humour has its penalties, for the man who has the same manner for the duchess as for the dairymaid is

Nothing Matters

apt to lay himself open to misconstruction at the hands of both sections of the community. Of course, it is only good manners to treat those in high places with a certain courtliness, lest they should feel uncomfortable, on the same principle that you sign yourself in a letter to an enemy, "Your most obedient servant." An acquaintance of mine was once talking to a personage who was not overburdened with intellect. A friend drew him aside and said:

"I noticed that when you were talking to that eminent immaterialist you showed a deference strangely out of keeping with your social views."

For the moment the other was taken aback.

"But," he explained, "it was not really snobbishness; it was just courtesy. I was only endeavouring to hide from him that I considered myself greatly his superior."

It is well to consider even the mistaken conventionalities of one's fellow-men, for to respect the prejudices of others is the first law of citizenship. Besides, it is very expensive to be a rebel; in reforming the world we are liable to hit our heads against the brick wall of human nature—and it is the head and not the wall that bleeds!

The actuality of life's tragedy is, of course, charged with humour. The records of the Old Bailey attest this. There was the case of the criminal who, on being asked by the judge if

Humour in Tragedy

he had anything to say why sentence of death should not be passed upon him, replied: "No; I am disgusted with the whole proceedings." Another, in a similar situation, on being asked whether he had any last request to make, said: "Well, I should like to learn the piano."

An instance of humour in tragedy (conscious or otherwise) came within my knowledge. I had constantly relieved the importunities of one who claimed to be a literary man, on the grounds, I subsequently discovered, that he addressed envelopes for an advertising firm. His constant plea with me was that he wanted to get a glass eye out of pawn. So frequent were his applications on this head that at last my secretary revolted. I received a letter couched in these terms:

"Sir,—Unless I receive ten shillings this evening, by ten o'clock my body will be floating down the Thames. On your head be it! I will call at the stage door!"

I was placed in a most invidious position, and told my secretary that he had better send out the ten shillings. At the end of the evening I thought of my friend.

"Did you send out the money to that deserving suicide?" I asked.

"No," replied my secretary; "I did not."

A horrible picture presented itself to my mind.

Nothing Matters

I felt myself guilty of manslaughter at the least. I was much relieved on leaving the stage door to find the importunate literary man outside, dancing a hornpipe to keep himself warm.

"Good evening, my friend," I said in cynical revulsion. "I thought you were in the Thames."

"Don't be flippant, sir," he said. "I did mean to submerge myself, but on gazing on the dark river my better feelings conquered, and I've come back—for the ten shillings." I think he deserved them.

One should be sparing in the use of humour.

Humour is the onion of the human salad; and, like the onion, it should only be half suspected. The very possession of this quality will prevent its too frequent use. Good wine should not be wasted; it should not be uncorked to those who gulp it down unthinkingly. In the same way it is dangerous to tell a story against yourself to those who have not humour, for they will always use it as evidence against you.

Flippancy is not humour. There are few things more tragic in life than to be a "funny man." Many a man learns to his cost that it is undesirable to stand on his head at the street corner too long.

Like every other natural force humour should be man's slave and not his master.

If humour is important as a guide in life, it

Humour in Tragedy

is no less potent a factor in art. In art humour is our best critic; it guards us from exaggeration. Tragedy, even more than comedy, needs this sweet sanity to hold us in check. Humour is the tingling sense which stays us from over-stepping the modesty of nature and prevents us from thinking out of tune; it is the delicate ear of the mind. It exercises the quality of restraint in tragedy; thus we avoid bathos. The man who pities himself is not an heroic figure. In art or in life one should never weep in the soup. In comedy humour guards us from degenerating into caricature. In the comedian humour is not so essential as it is in the tragedian, for a funny personality, an awkward gait, an impediment of speech are often a substitute for comic genius. We are so liable to mistake for a gift of God what is, after all, only a visitation of providence.

Humour in comedy guards us from degenerating into buffoonery. This, of course, applies also to pictorial art. Nor should one allow one's sense of humour to run away with one's sense of the fitness of things. The originators of Futurism are overburdened with humour. They have too much—their disciples too little. A great deal of nonsense is always talked about New Art; there is no such thing as new art. There are always two kinds of art—good art and bad art. There is a certain difference between Art and Science.

Nothing Matters

Science is always advancing upward in a straight line—Art moves in a circle, or shall I say, as a fountain which, when it reaches its height, drops back into its basin and thence rises again.

There has been no " advance," for instance, in the art of sculpture ; that of the Greeks cannot be excelled. Literature has not " advanced " ; it is simply good or bad. The same may be said of acting.

To hold the mirror up to Nature, at the flattering angle of Art, that is the business of the actor—according to Shakespeare, whose own textbook was Nature. In tragedy we had, of course, the stentorian actor whose vocality was his chief stock-in-trade ; but the merely outwardly equipped player has no abiding influence with the public nowadays. The critical will often be captured by technique, but the public have an intuition beyond the outward flourishes of artifice. In acting, the brain and the heart must be as the negative and positive poles. Instructed by the book of Nature an actor should be able to play comedy or tragedy at will. Novelli, the Italian actor, for instance, will play a tragedy and a farce on the same night. David Garrick and Edmund Kean were said to be equally good in comedy and in tragedy. Apart from the artistic advantage of the actor varying his part, there is one aspect which is not, I think, sufficiently

Humour in Tragedy

recognised—the exercise of dramatic art as a pleasure to the player—a pleasure quite as great, I venture to think, as grouse-shooting, horse-racing, football, fly-fishing, or even bezique. It is certainly a most healthy occupation, probably because it engages the body and the mind at the same time. Especially is it a privilege to be prized above the substantial reward that is often bountifully bestowed upon us, to recite the words of Shakespeare upon the stage ; to the actor who is lifted above himself in giving utterance to the poet's soaring words, it is a joy to be upborne on their wings into the heights of imagination and emotion, to live for the time being in the rarer ether half-way between earth and heaven as in an airship of the mind. In his highest moments, too, it may be his privilege to communicate his own ecstasy to his listeners. To speak the words of Hamlet, for example, with all the illusion and the mystery of the scene, is something to live for.

During the war it is but natural that classic drama, in common with all the arts, should be in abeyance ; for art is essentially a pastime of peace—it can only flourish in repose.

The theatre, which had become a strong factor in the life of a nation, is now chiefly devoted to frankly funny plays and *revues*. We try to forget the horrors of the day in the frivolities of

Nothing Matters

the night. Shakespeare is for the time being under a war-cloud. Nor is one curious as to serious music or pictorial art, or the art of the sculptor. What occupation would there be to-day for Benvenuto Cellini, unless it were to chase designs on explosive shells?

To-day we all realise our infinite insignificance. We feel there is something more important than ourselves, and that is the nation. There is something more important than the nation, and that is the world. There is something more important than the present, and that is Eternity. For that Eternity we are fighting. With the advent of peace, Art will once more come into its own.

The actor's art, which has many drawbacks, has also its great compensations.

The actor, like the orator, is twice blessed, for he not only gives but takes from his hearers —he draws their vitality into himself and gives it back again. I am sure that this " give and take " exists between the actor and his audience. The actor has this advantage over the orator— that he is not rendered self-conscious by speaking his own words. I suppose all but the greatest public speakers feel this self-consciousness. The orator is apt to be hampered by his own periods, whereas the actor is not ashamed to be inspired by those of the poet, and, carried away by their

Humour in Tragedy

eloquence, he can throw himself subjectively into the passion and nobility of the scene. And so he lives in his artistic life the lives of great and noble men. It would be interesting to debate to what extent this exercise influences his own life and develops his own character—but that is another story.

In confirmation of what I have said of the psychology of audiences, I may recall a saying of Mr. Gladstone's: " The work of the orator is cast in the mould offered by the mind of his hearers. It is an influence principally received from his audience (so to speak) in vapour, which he pours back upon them in flood." Mr. Gladstone was himself, of course, a great orator, and had that power of self-excitation which made the waves of his passion vibrate in his audience—he had, in fact, the histrionic gift in an extraordinary degree. If that statesman lacked something of ultimate greatness it was that he fell short of the humour with which his great opponent Disraeli was gifted so supremely. It was with the shafts of his humour that Disraeli made his great effects with deadly certainty.

It is with humour that a truth is often thrust home more poignantly than by the most vehement invective. In literature the quality of humour is of transcendent value; by its light should one always correct one's proof-sheets.

Nothing Matters

Especially is it valuable in the literature of our own day.

Our quick life calls for greater brevity of expression; there is no room for the rolling periods of our forefathers in these days of hurry and stress, of telegraphs and telephones and taxis. The modern author will often concentrate in one vibrant passage of humour the long-drawn rhetoric with which his predecessors would have embroidered the same thought.

It has been said that no great man ever had a sense of humour. I imagine this dictum emanates from those who were themselves devoid of the quality they despised. In literature certainly it is difficult to find any really great writer who does not possess humour, unless it be the solitary case of Milton; but it may be claimed that he would have been the greater for its possession—even as Shakespeare was.

The humour of tragedy is strongly evidenced in the irony of the Greek dramatists. Sophocles must have possessed it in a supreme degree. Had the author of *Œdipus* not been so blessed he assuredly could not have shown us perhaps the most tremendous of all tragedies without crossing the borderland that separates awe from disgust. In the presence of a great work of art we must exclaim " Ah ! "—never " Ugh ! " In *Œdipus* the audience is in the secret of the author,

Humour in Tragedy

who withholds it from his hero. A distinguished writer once said to me (and it is an admirable rule for the aspiring dramatist): "The moment the actors on the stage know as much as the audience, the play is at an end." The Greek tragic writers, in their irony, were perhaps more guided by humour than were the writers of comedy; Aristophanes, I venture to think, was more remarkable for his wit than his humour, just as Molière was greater in humour than in wit. Dante, who relegated several of his living contemporaries to Hell, surely showed signs of humour in tragedy. In Scripture there are, of course, isolated instances of humour. Ibsen is charged with humour. Notably do we find it in Dr. Stockmann in the last act of *The Enemy of the People*. In the pitiful tragedy of poor Stockmann's failure our hero still remains tactlessly buoyant. Bleeding and torn, he cries, "A man should never put on his best trousers when he goes out to battle for truth and freedom!" While we laugh, we have a supreme pity for this battered altruist.

Dickens's muse, again, overflows with humour. Witness the death of Barkis. Three of the greatest creations of the world's humour are really tragic—Micawber, Colonel Newcome, and Don Quixote. None of these characters has humour —their appeal to our sense of humour consists

Nothing Matters

in their lack of it. Mr. Micawber is, of course, tragically devoid of humour; he takes himself seriously in every comic situation in which he is placed. It is the paradox that makes us laugh. Colonel Newcome, though observed with a tender humour by Thackeray, is himself lacking in that quality. The pathos of the character is that he does not descend to self-pity. How infinitely touching is the scene in which the Colonel attempts to sing "Wapping Old Stairs." By the by, what a sublime touch of humour is the "Adsum" in the Colonel's death. In Don Quixote, again, the infinite humour is entirely unconscious. Without it there would be no tragedy in these three masterpieces of character. One might multiply such instances indefinitely; but in the brief traffic of a lecture I must be sparing. I will content myself with one great example.

Of all writers he whose works are most charged with an all-informing, all-pervading humour, is William Shakespeare, alike in his comic as in his tragic creations. In *Hamlet*, for instance, the firmament of tragedy is made blacker by the jewels of humour with which it is bestarred. The first words Hamlet sighs forth are in the nature of a pun:

"A little more than kin and less than kind."

The King proceeds: "How is it that the

Humour in Tragedy

clouds still hang on you?" "Not so, my lord; I am too much in the sun," says Hamlet, toying with grief. Again, after the ghost leaves, Hamlet, in a tornado of passionate verbiage, gives way to humour. Then he proceeds to think too precisely on the event. But for his humour Hamlet would have killed the King in the first act. It was this very humour, this seeing all sides of a question, which may be said to have been Hamlet's undoing.

"There is nothing either good or bad, but thinking makes it so."

He cannot help dallying with humour in his searching cross-examination of Polonius. Again with Rosencrantz and Guildenstern does he indulge his elfin spirit; then away runs his imagination to delight in a dissertation on the players. His contemplation of life becomes almost more important than its actuality—he himself has his fling at the actor's art. Immediately after, in the speech beginning, "Oh, what a rogue and peasant slave am I," he stops to laugh at himself, and the bloody business of life. He sees too much, and, seeing too much, he does too little. "A great man's memory," he says in the acted murder scene, "may outlive his life by half a year, *but by 'r Lady he must build churches then!*" Then, instead of killing the

Nothing Matters

King right off, he revels in the mimicry of madness. His imagination, with his humour in attendance, is his Nemesis. Even in the graveyard scene he must, perforce, sit on the perilous safety-valve of his humour. He knows his own weakness. *His* humour unhappily did not stop short at himself. There is almost a divinity in his blague when he addresses Yorick's skull. He has too much of what the slaughtering conqueror has too little. Even in dying, he breaks into a sweet irony of humour, in meeting the " fell serjeant Death." " The rest is silence." Hamlet ends as he began, in humour's minor key. Here is the humour of tragedy with a vengeance. Poor Hamlet, too much humour hadst thou for this harsh world!

But, indeed, most of Shakespeare's great male creations are gilded with humour, conscious or unconscious; notably Shylock, Falconbridge, Caliban, Timon of Athens, Henry V., Hotspur, Marc Antony, and the two Richards. Richard II. is, I cannot help thinking, the literary progenitor of Hamlet. In both these characters there is much of Shakespeare's own contemplative, versatile nature. There is in both of these the same wayward humour that peeps out in Feste, the fool of *Twelfth Night*. Here, again, in a comedy character is the wood note, sad and wild, of Shakespeare. " Come away, come away,

Humour in Tragedy

Death," sings the Clown: it is humour in tragedy and tragedy in humour.

Throughout *Richard II.* there is this same melodic humour. When Richard is utterly crest-fallen and self-vanquished he revels in humour, laughing at himself and his state. After railing against the false friends who have betrayed him, he sinks down upon the grass to make sport of the divine right of kings. Here assuredly again we have the importance of humour in tragedy.

Macbeth, another great tragic figure, is, of course, devoid of those glimpses of humour so dear to the poet. But we have again a notable instance of the importance of humour in tragedy in the introduction of the drunken porter, to add a deeper hue to the terror of the scene of murder that follows.

There is another example in *Romeo and Juliet* of the value of humour in tragedy. I refer to the death of Mercutio. Speaking of his death wound, Mercutio says, " 'Tis not so deep as a well, nor so wide as a church door; but 'tis enough; 'twill serve; ask for me to-morrow and you shall find me a grave man. I am peppered, I warrant, for this world. A plague o' both your houses! They have made worms' meat of me. I have it, and soundly too; your houses!" And Mercutio dies with a laugh in his throat. I may also instance the tragic fall

Nothing Matters

of that emperor of humorists, Falstaff. After the King had degraded Falstaff publicly, and had gone on his way, the fat knight, whose life was wrecked, merely turned to Master Shallow and said, " Master Shallow, I owe you a thousand pound." Then, too, we have Marc Antony, whom Shakespeare endows with rich humour. In *Antony and Cleopatra* he, of course, has the joy of life to a criminal extent.

In the play of *Antony and Cleopatra* I may note in passing a little touch of realism that only one of Shakespeare's delicate humour could suggest. When Cleopatra has breathed her last breath, Charmian says:

> " So fare thee well.
> Now boast thee, death ; in thy possession lies
> A lass unparallel'd. Downy windows, close ;
> And golden Phœbus never be beheld
> Of eyes again so royal ! *Your crown's awry ;*
> I'll mend it, and then play."

"Your crown's awry "—that is a true Shakespearean touch. It reminds one of Dickens's Fagin, who, while he was awaiting sentence of death, fell to counting the iron spikes in the court and wondered how the head of one had been broken off, and whether they would mend it, or leave it as it was. And in the play of Cæsar, what an understanding of the mob does Antony reveal

Humour in Tragedy

in his dealing with the motley crowd. To Brutus, to Cassius, and to Cæsar, Shakespeare purposely denies the gift of humour, though Casca (a kind of Labouchere of the period) has it richly. Indeed, Shakespeare appears to have a grudge against the conqueror Cæsar, whom he makes a conceited and bombastic person, good enough perhaps to conquer the world, but sitting intellectually below the salt of humour. This hatred of the tyrant by the poet is not unnatural.

After Cæsar's death Antony lovingly mourns over his dead friend; the conspirators turn on him; but for all the passion of his grief, above Antony's head there hovers the imp Humour, and, aided by this second consciousness, he wilily plays upon the murderers of Cæsar as he subsequently plays like an artist upon his instrument the mob, or as an adroit conductor will dominate his orchestra. Antony wins by humour; while Brutus wins by the lack of it, for he deceives even himself—he wins by blind steadfastness of purpose—by character, and character is destiny. Shakespeare, the all-sided, recognised and admired the strong single-purposed man of action.

This brings me to the question as to the possession or non-possession of humour by great men. As I suggested a little while ago, humour may be a help or a clog in life. Many great men have been without it. I think it may be broadly

Nothing Matters

stated that men of action, the great destroyers, the men who take, are as a rule devoid of humour; while men of imagination and contemplation, those who create, who give, *have* the gift of humour.

Among those pre-eminently gifted with humour are Abraham Lincoln, Disraeli, Goethe and Heine, the late Lord Salisbury, Arthur Balfour, Dickens, Thackeray, Fielding, Shakespeare, Queen Elizabeth, Henry VIII., Charles II., Dr. Johnson, Charles Lamb, Emerson and Byron.

I could enlarge upon this theme until *your* eyelids would no longer wag. But I will content myself with contrasting as typical examples of the yea and nay of humour two of the world's greatest men—Shakespeare and Napoleon: the arch-creator and the arch-destroyer. I take it that the greatness of a man must be gauged by his output for good—the measure of his greatness is, in fact, in proportion to what he gives to the world, his lack of greatness by what he takes or destroys. Shakespeare gave an abiding joy, one that will contribute to the happiness, the education, and the ennobling of mankind throughout the ages, " in states unborn and accents yet unknown "; Napoleon, on the other hand, took from mankind millions of lives and set humanity wailing. What of his work remains behind ? The flower of France was destroyed and the French race is suffering to

Humour in Tragedy

this day from the depletion it suffered at the hands of a would-be ruler of the globe. Shakespeare enriched the world, Napoleon impoverished it. Which is the greater, the giver or the taker-away? The poet or the emperor? The man of humour or the man of worldly ambition? Shakespeare with humour, or Napoleon without? Napoleon was somewhat of a vulgarian with a mighty brain—and sane to the core; but he lacked humour. He may have had the imagination to visualise the terrors of the war and the suffering he inflicted on mankind—he did not possess the humour to ask himself: "Is this worth while?" And he might have been the head of a great republic with a government which should have been the model of the world. As it was, he died in exile and misery; while Shakespeare, who was content to employ his genius in comparative obscurity, died at Stratford-on-Avon in sweet content, let us hope. The game is not worth the candle of fame.

Is it not time that the great ones of the earth learned the lesson, or were made to learn the lesson, which the religion of humanity teaches?

It is difficult to think of the Emperor Napoleon without thinking of the Emperor Wilhelm. The resemblance between these two great criminals is not one of person, for two men could hardly be more unlike; the likeness is in their monstrous ambition.

Nothing Matters

Before the war Wilhelm II. had always appeared to me as the best thing made in modern Germany—not the Germany whose rich soul gave us philosophy, and freedom of thought, and great music; but the modern, materialistic Germany — the Germany laid low by luxury. To the *nouveau riche* nothing is so disconcerting as luxury. They say that decadence is a product of peace. Is this wholly true? In modern Germany the foul weed of decadence has grown with the growth of a military materialism. They say that war is noble. Has the military spirit ennobled the German nation? No; it has murdered the soul of Germany.

The Kaiser seemed a link with the old Germany—the Germany of Goethe, of Beethoven, and of Wagner. He appeared to be an idealist; his eloquence, the man himself, seemed to possess a certain ethical glow, a mediæval splendour of feudal egoism—a sincere " I am I." He seemed a true believer in himself and his God whom he made in his own image. Every man has the God he deserves. Had he had the imagination to see that his true *rôle* was to place himself in front of mankind as the champion of peace he would have gained an immortality above all conquerors; he would have gone down the ages as the temporal saviour of mankind. But the temptation of earthly glory was too great.

Humour in Tragedy

The mighty machine into which he conjured the spirit of the Devil was built up—his but the finger to press the button, and hey, presto! the world is in ruins. "How oft the sight of means to do ill deeds makes ill deeds done!" Now, whether he win or lose, he will go down the centuries as the greatest slaughterer of the world. What a terrible picture of this stricken man the mind conjures up: we can see him wavering between the ambition of eternal peace and the ambition of world-conquest. I have no doubt that he was persuaded that what he did was for the glory, the greatness of Hohenzollernised Germany.

Between Wilhelm and his predecessor, Frederick the Great, there is a certain affinity. That remarkable monarch once spoke these words of frank and brutal self-revelation (I am quoting from Macaulay): "Ambition, interest, the desire of making people talk about me, carried the day; and I decided for war." Who could contemplate the self-wrought carnage of this war, and see the lives of millions sacrificed without taking his own? What is the force that enables this man to distribute Iron Crosses; to adjust his unhallowed halo of divine right? What is it that enables him still to pose as the vice-regent of God? I know what it is—it is the calm of a madman. It is the negation of humour. He must still go forward, for the way back is barred by the dead.

> " I am in blood stepp'd in so far
> That, should I wade no more,
> Returning were as tedious as go o'er."

We must fight on, for our enemy is Cæsarism—Kaiserism. It behoves every man and every woman in this land to lend a hand to help to conquer the enemy, for if the Allies were beaten then would prevail the most terrible tyranny known to mankind—the Prussifaction of the world. The soul of Germany lies stricken—the German *Geist* is in its death-throes. The Kaiser lacked the divine humour—that humour which divine right cannot confer—to know the spirit of England. Yet what a little, little dividing line there is between victory and glory on the one hand, and defeat and disgrace on the other. Let us be frank. Had it not been for the intervention of England, the German Emperor might be acclaimed as the greatest man in history; only one little human speck put out of gear the great war machine, the most wonderful piece of work the ingenuity of mankind has ever achieved, on which not only the genius but the resources, the wealth accumulated by the toiling commerce of Germany, have been lavished. On this machine hundreds of millions have been squandered. If

Humour in Tragedy

half this wasted ingenuity, half this spilt genius, had been devoted to the making of a peace machine, the peace of the world would have been assured for the next five hundred years—and by that time humanity would have lost the habit of war.

That peace must be attained. That is why we must fight on. That is why the civilised world must not submit to peace till the machine is ground to dust. We often hear the cry: " War will never cease; man is an animal, and will always fight." True, man is an animal—he was a man-eating animal; but cannibalism is no longer practised, and war, as fought to-day, is as fierce and as foul as cannibalism.

Now we are assured that our remote ancestors had tails. They were, no doubt, as proud of these appendages as we are of more glittering decorations. Gradually these tails fell into disuse; men would be ashamed to wear them to-day; let us hope the day will come when they will be equally ashamed to kill their fellow-men. Let us make haste to prepare for the Day. I was lately talking with a friend. " After the war," said he, " nothing will change. We shall just sit under a tree, smoke a pipe, and say, ' Thank God, that's over ! ' And all will be the same again." I hope that may not be so. Let there be no peace-slackers !

It is not force only, nor force mainly, that

Nothing Matters

rules the world. Look at South Africa—contrast its recent history with that of Alsace-Lorraine. It was thought by the thoughtless that the Boers would be the enemies of England—that they were implacable; but, lo and behold! ten years of English rule made them brothers. Why? Because England, after conquering, gave them what they needed: that is England's genius—to rule other people by understanding, by sympathy, by humour. What has the culture of the Prussian drill-sergeant done to placate or to subjugate Alsace? Forty years have not availed! The Alsatian peasant children say their multiplication tables in German, but they say their prayers in French.

There was one moment of this war which was tinged with a divine humour. It was at Christmas time in the first year of the war, when the British and German soldiers fraternised. They remembered they were brothers, and forgot to be fratricides. Had this spirit animated the nations, this war would not have been.

But even in this great tragedy the importance of humour has asserted itself, for surely it may be said that the force which more than any other has kept up the spirit of our soldiers at the Front has been their unconquerable humour. It is this national gift which has constantly baffled and disconcerted the enemy hordes. While they

Humour in Tragedy

were singing the "Hymn of Hate," the British were singing "Tipperary." But for this good humour the tragedy of those trenches would have been intolerable.

It is this spirit that has enabled the men at the Front to preserve their calm. To be calm in crisis—that is the test of men. Let us hope that this spirit will prevail at peace-time among the nations who are vindicating the freedom of the world. Meantime, we must fight on.

There could only have been one greater tragedy than the war—the greater tragedy would have been if England had not joined in the war. The proudest thing England has ever done is to have fought for the ideal of the world's right. She went into the war with clean hands, as she may elect to go out with empty. In that great hour it is Britain that should be destined to take the lead among the nations; it is those who have, with noble calm, guided her in the tremendous times through which we are now passing, who will guide us in the hour of victory with a moderation which is stronger than violence. And when the hour strikes, let the note be solemn. Let us have the humour to go forth to greet the Angel of Peace with anthems rather than with comic songs. Half a century ago Emerson wrote these words of England—they are almost prophetic of the England of to-day:

Nothing Matters

"I see her not dispirited, not weak, but well remembering that she has seen dark days before; indeed, with a kind of instinct that she sees a little better in a cloudy day, and that in storm of battle and calamity she has a secret vigour, and a pulse like cannon. I see her in her old age, not decrepit but young, and still daring to believe in her power of endurance and expansion. Seeing this, I say *all* hail! Mother of nations, Mother of heroes! With strength still equal to the time, still wise to entertain and swift to execute the policy which the mind and heart of mankind require at the present hour, and thus only hospitable to the foreigner, and truly a home to the thoughtful and generous, who are born in the soil. So be it! So let it be!"

Should victory be on the side of right, there is one more war ahead of us—and only one—the war for peace; there is only one cause henceforth worth shedding blood for—the cause of peace. As in peace it behoved us to prepare for war, so in war does it behove us to prepare for peace. Let us not be taken unawares, for the end of the war may be as sudden as its beginning.

How can that abiding peace be obtained? By the union of the workers of all countries, with the guidance and the inspiration of the master-spirits of the world. I know that many injustices have been committed even during this war in the sacred name of organised Labour, disorganised. Democracy is a terrific force to-day;

Humour in Tragedy

rightly used and ethically guided, it has it in its power to put an end to all wars by a holy strike. Let the men and women workers of all nations cry, "We forbid war!" Aye, let the women make their voices heard. It will be the women's hour! As they have been the ministering angels during the war, so let them be the ministering angels of peace hereafter. Meantime, we must fight on.

It is those who most love peace who are most determined to pursue this war to its bitter end. It is our soil, our soul, our all we are fighting for. Out of evil cometh good; let not the fair fields of France and Belgium have been soaked in vain with our brothers' blood; let not the virgin soil of Russia have been ravished unavenged and unconsoled. Let us hope that out of the agony and bloody sweat of this war may spring a nobler, a greater humanity. The womb of misfortune should bring forth great men—may it send us some great spiritual Dictator whose call the world shall follow. May there rally to him the thinkers, the scientists, the preachers, the teachers, the artists, the poets of the world! The sword has been mightier than the pen, but from the pens of poets shall be forged a sword mightier than all—the sword of Justice and of Peace. We cannot clearly hear the message yet, for the sound of the anvil drowns the song of the poet. But

Nothing Matters

faintly it is humming in our ears. His song is to the workers of the world—he is calling on them in every clime, in every country, of whatsoever religion, to join in the great clamour that there shall be no more wars—no, not for the vanity of kings, nor for the greed of gold. Led by this new Conqueror, let the toiling millions of all countries join together singing in one great choir the new hymn of humanity; and amid the din of an awakened world I seem to hear the phantom bells of Rheims ringing forth their message of Peace and Goodwill.

Library
Brevard Junior College
Cocoa, Florida